THE FOLGER LIBRARY
SHAKESPEARE

Designed to make Shakespeare's classic plays available to the general reader, each edition contains a reliable text with modernized spelling and punctuation, scene-by-scene plot summaries, and explanatory notes clarifying obscure and obsolete expressions. An interpretive essay and accounts of Shakespeare's life and theater form an instructive preface to each play.

Louis B. Wright, General Editor, was the Director of the Folger Shakespeare Library from 1948 until his retirement in 1968. He is the author of *Middle-Class Culture in Elizabethan England, Religion and Empire, Shakespeare for Everyman,* and many other books and essays on the history and literature of the Tudor and Stuart periods.

Virginia Lamar, Assistant Editor, served as research assistant to the Director and Executive Secretary of the Folger Shakespeare Library from 1946 until her death in 1968. She is the author of *English Dress in the Age of Shakespeare* and *Travel and Roads in England,* and coeditor of William Strachey's *Historie of Travell into Virginia Britania.*

The Folger Shakespeare Library

GENERAL EDITOR

LOUIS B. WRIGHT

Director, Folger Shakespeare Library, 1948–1968

ASSISTANT EDITOR

VIRGINIA A. LaMAR

Executive Secretary, Folger Shakespeare Library, 1946–1968

The Folger Library General Reader's Shakespeare

SHAKESPEARE'S
POEMS

PUBLISHED BY POCKET BOOKS NEW YORK

Preface

This edition of *Shakespeare's Poems* is designed to provide a readable text of Shakespeare's narrative poems and other verse exclusive of the sonnets, which are published separately in another volume in this series. In the centuries since Shakespeare, many changes have occurred in the meanings of words, and some clarification of Shakespeare's vocabulary may be helpful. To provide the reader with necessary notes in the most accessible format, we have placed them on the pages facing the text that they explain. We have tried to make them as brief and simple as possible. Preliminary to the text we have also included a brief statement of essential information about Shakespeare and his stage. Readers desiring more detailed information should refer to the books suggested in the references, and if still further information is needed, the bibliographies in those books will provide the necessary clues to the literature of the subject.

All illustrations are from material in the Folger Library collections.

L. B. W.
V. A. L.

February 22, 1968

CONTENTS

the Globe, the burgers organized a syndicate composed of the leading . . . the dramatic company, of which Shakespeare was a partner

Shakespeare's Poems

TO UNDERSTAND *Venus and Adonis* and *Lucrece* it is necessary to understand the literary fashions of Shakespeare's day. As a young aspirant to a literary reputation, Shakespeare felt compelled to write something that would be considered "literature." Although he was making a reputation as a writer of plays, dramatic pieces in his time had hardly more claim to be called literature than do radio or television scripts today. To establish himself as a literary figure, Shakespeare had to write something that would be approved by the literary public. Narrative, lyric, or epic poetry would meet this requirement. Consequently, Shakespeare turned his hand to narrative verse and produced two poems that immediately found favor with the public: *Venus and Adonis* (1593) followed a year later by *Lucrece* (1594). Having proved himself a "poet" in the accepted tradition, he could now go on about the business of being a productive playwright. Furthermore, according to tradition, he received not only recognition but a substantial financial reward from the Earl of Southampton to whom he dedicated both poems.

VENVS
AND ADONIS

Vilia miretur vulgus: mihi flauus Apollo
Pocula Castalia plena ministret aqua.

LONDON
Imprinted by Richard Field, and are to be sold at
the signe of the white Greyhound in
Paules Church-yard.
1593.

The title page of the first edition of *Venus and Adonis* (1593).
Courtesy, the Bodleian Library.

In 1593, when Shakespeare wrote his dedication to *Venus and Adonis,* Southampton was a dashing courtier, not quite twenty years old, in great favor at the Court of Queen Elizabeth. The author himself was only twenty-nine. A rising young nobleman of Southampton's type was precisely the sort to whom an aspiring author might dedicate an amorous poem written in the Ovidian manner. Evidently Southampton was pleased, because the next year Shakespeare dedicated to him his second long poem, *Lucrece.* According to Nicholas Rowe, writing in 1709, Southampton proved a generous patron and "at one time gave him [Shakespeare] a thousand pounds to enable him to go through with a purchase which he heard he had a mind to." As Sir Edmund Chambers points out, this amount is clearly an exaggeration, but Southampton obviously found Shakespeare's dedications pleasing to his vanity. Furthermore, he doubtless found the subject matter of *Venus and Adonis* congenial to his taste.

In the dedication of *Venus and Adonis,* Shakespeare describes his poem as "the first heir of my invention," a phrase which has bothered some critics because he had already written plays. Obviously the author is simply discounting his playwriting as of no moment; he is saying that this poem is his first literary production.

To get *Venus and Adonis* into print, Shakespeare sought out Richard Field, a Stratford man who had come up to London and established himself as a printer. Field registered the poem with the Stationers' Company on April 18, 1593, and published it in quarto size soon thereafter. This first quarto version was well printed and is the basic text used for all later editions, including the present. The poem was immediately popular and went through at least sixteen editions by 1640. Some of the later editions are printed in octavo size, but for convenience all editions are usually listed as "quartos."

The success of *Venus and Adonis* was encouraging, and in 1594 Shakespeare had Field bring out *Lucrece* in quarto. Though the title page simply called the poem *Lucrece*, the running title over the pages of the text was given as "The Rape of Lucrece." *Lucrece* also proved a popular success and went through eight editions by 1640. As in the case of *Venus and Adonis*, the first quarto of *Lucrece* is the basis for all later editions.

The two poems, *Venus and Adonis* and *Lucrece*, treat love and passion from different points of view and apparently were designed for contrast. The first deals with love in a light, almost comic, vein, even though young Adonis does die in the end. As F. T. Prince observes in the new Arden edition of the *Poems*, "The fate of a youth who, having been slain by a wild boar, evaporates into air, and whose blood turns into a flower, to be plucked and worn by a goddess in her bosom, is not intended to rouse tragic emotions. The retention of this fairy-tale detail from Ovid is only the most obvious of Shakespeare's innumerable devices to make his story light as a bubble and to keep it floating." *Lucrece*, on the other hand, treats the darker side of passion in a way more fitting for a tragic drama than a narrative poem. The soliloquy-like meditations of Tarquin and the declamatory speeches of Lucrece sound as

LVCRECE.

AN CHO RA SPES.

LONDON.
Printed by Richard Field, for Iohn Harrison, and are
to be sold at the signe of the white Greyhound.
in Paules Churh-yard. 1594.

The title page of the first edition of *Lucrece* (1594) printed,
like *Venus and Adonis* the year before, by Shakespeare's Stratford
friend, Richard Field.

if the author had fashioned them for dramatic utterance. It may be significant that the grim tragedy of *Titus Andronicus* and *Lucrece* both saw their first publication in the same year, 1594. The light mood of *Venus and Adonis* had temporarily vanished.

Shakespeare's narrative poems represent a fashion in verse adaptation of classical legend popular in the later years of the sixteenth century. The erotic behavior of the gods on Olympus and of other figures in classical mythology, as revealed by Ovid, appealed particularly to the Elizabethans. Thomas Lodge published in 1589 a verse narrative, *Scilla's Metamorphosis, Interlaced with the Unfortunate Love of Glaucus* which appeared again in 1610 with a variant title, *A Most Pleasant History of Glaucus and Scilla*. Christopher Marlowe, who died on May 30, 1593, left an unfinished poem, *Hero and Leander,* which had an even more erotic appeal than *Venus and Adonis*. Other contemporaries of Shakespeare were diligently reading their copies of Arthur Golding's translation of Ovid's *Metamorphoses* or, if they were well-Latined, reading Ovid in the original. Golding had published the first four books of the *Metamorphoses* in 1565 and followed this in 1567 with *The XV Books of P. Ovidius Naso, Entitled Metamorphosis*. The latter work had at least seven editions by 1612. Ovid in the original, of course, was standard reading in the grammar schools, and Shakespeare as a schoolboy had learned his Ovid well. Throughout his poems and plays occur innumerable echoes of Ovid. The source for Shakespeare's *Venus and Adonis* is the

Metamorphoses. The poet telescoped material from two episodes, Venus' encounter with Adonis and the nymph Salmacis' infatuation with Hermaphroditus.

Golding's Ovid has Venus dally with Adonis, caress him, warn him against the dangers of boar hunting, and depart in her swan-drawn chariot. In the next episode a nymph, Salmacis, spies young Hermaphroditus bathing in a pool and is instantly carried away by passion for the handsome lad. She plunges into the pool, wrestles him to shore, and, though he resists for a time, the gods above answer Salmacis' prayer for Hermaphroditus' love. He surrenders so that, as Golding phrased it, "The bodies of them twain/ Were mixt and joined both in one."

For his own purposes, Shakespeare changed the story and concentrated the entire love encounter between Venus and Adonis. Furthermore, he made Adonis resist to the end, leaving the goddess of love disconsolate. This new treatment of the legend was one that might have appealed to a youth like the handsome and spoiled Southampton. Already pursued by women himself, he must have been amused and pleased at Adonis' capacity to resist the wiles of a pursuing woman. Shakespeare makes Venus' importunity somewhat ridiculous, and his interpretation of the tale undoubtedly entertained brash young courtiers of the day. Theirs was a man's world, and they took their love where they found it—or, with callous arrogance, left despairing damsels unsolaced. They could laugh at Shakespeare's Venus and remember similar situations in their own experience.

The. xv. Bookes

of P. Ouidius Naso, entytuled
Metamorphosis, translated oute of
Latin into English meeter, by Ar-
thur Golding Gentleman,
A worke very pleasaunt
and delectable.

With skill, heede, and iudgement, this worke must be read,
For else to the Reader it standes in small stead.

15 67

Imprynted at London, by
Willyam Seres.

The title page of Arthur Golding's translation of Ovid's
Metamorphoses (1567).

In his *History of English Literature* a French scholar, Emile Legouis, points out that in *Venus and Adonis* Shakespeare eliminates most of the classical mythology and substitutes a realistic situation: "His goddess is a woman skilled in love-making and ravaged by passion, and in Adonis we already have the young sport-loving Englishman, annoyed and fretted by the pursuit of a beautiful amorous courtesan whose sensuality is unbounded and who retains no prestige of divinity."

Although only a fanatically earnest symbolist or allegorist can find any deep moral significance in *Venus and Adonis,* the poem does have foreshadowings of meaningful passages in later plays and in the *Sonnets.* Venus' arguments to Adonis remind one of the so-called "procreation" sonnets:

"Torches are made to light, jewels to wear,
  Dainties to taste, fresh beauty for the use,
  Herbs for their smell, and sappy plants to bear;
  Things growing to themselves are growth's abuse.
  Seeds spring from seeds and beauty breedeth beauty;
  Thou wast begot; to get it is thy duty.

"Upon the earth's increase why shouldst thou feed,
  Unless the earth with thy increase be fed?
  By law of nature thou art bound to breed,
  That thine may live when thou thyself art dead;
  And so in spite of death thou dost survive,
  In that thy likeness still is left alive."

                    [*Venus and Adonis,* ll. 163–174.]

Further similarities to the *Sonnets* appear in other stanzas.

Later in the poem, the contrast between love and lust, the burden of Adonis' rebuttal of Venus' plea, reminds one of the same theme that appears from time to time in the plays, as early as *Romeo and Juliet* and later in *Measure for Measure*:

"Call it not love, for love to heaven is fled
　Since sweating Lust on earth usurped his name;
　Under whose simple semblance he hath fed
　Upon fresh beauty, blotting it with blame;
　Which the hot tyrant stains and soon bereaves,
　As caterpillars do the tender leaves.

"Love comforteth like sunshine after rain,
　But Lust's effect is tempest after sun;
　Love's gentle spring doth always fresh remain,
　Lust's winter comes ere summer half be done;
　Love surfeits not, Lust like a glutton dies;
　Love is all truth, Lust full of forged lies."
　　　　　　　　[*Venus and Adonis*, ll. 793–804.]

In *Othello* (III, iii), the passage ". . . and when I love thee not/ Chaos is come again" reminds one of Venus' lament over Adonis:

　"For he being dead, with him is beauty slain,
　　And, beauty dead, black chaos comes again."

Other similarities in Shakespeare's later work indicate the power of phrasing that he was already mastering in this early poem.

Critics have long acclaimed the poetic imagery in the verses describing the jennet and the stallion and the poor trembling hare. Shakespeare brought from the woods and fields of Warwickshire a fund of memories of outdoor life that he utilized effectively in his poems as well as in his later plays.

In *Lucrece,* Shakespeare again took material from Ovid, this time from the *Fasti,* which he must have read in the original Latin. He also drew upon Livy for details, and he might have used other sources for a legend that had been constantly retold. Chaucer in *The Legend of Good Women* provides a version of Lucrece "As seyth Ovyde and Titus Lyvius." William Painter took from Livy the story which he included in *The Palace of Pleasure* (1566).

Shakespeare's version of the Lucrece tale follows somewhat the pattern of an old type of poetic "complaint" that gained popularity with *The Mirror for Magistrates* (1559). In this collection of verse "tragedies," the ghosts of various figures from history report their sad state and the conditions that brought them to such a sorry pass. Although *Lucrece* is more sophisticated and less conventionally designed than the older "complaints," it nevertheless shows an affinity with the type. Indeed, a number of poems more or less contemporary with *Lucrece* exemplify a new form of complaint influenced by Ovid. In 1592, Samuel Daniel published *The Complaint of Rosamond* which stimulated a renewed interest in this form of narrative verse.

The modern reader finds Shakespeare's *Lucrece* tedious and tiresome. Someone has said that the poet is more interested in Tarquin's soul than in Lucrece's body. At any rate, Shakespeare has Tarquin give a lengthy meditation before committing his crime and an even more lengthy meditation on his guilt afterward. But it is Lucrece who bores us most with her lamentations. The impact of her declamations upon most readers is succinctly described by F. T. Prince in his introduction in the new Arden edition of the *Poems:* "The greatest weakness of Shakespeare's *Lucrece* is . . . her remorseless eloquence. In Ovid Lucrece does not even plead with Tarquin; but Shakespeare makes her start an argument which might have continued indefinitely if the ravisher had not cut it short. After her violation, Lucrece loses our sympathy exactly in proportion as she gives tongue."

Despite its obvious weaknesses, *Lucrece* has passages that show a powerful feeling for imagery and a deepening sense of tragedy. The poem reflects the somber cast of *Titus Andronicus* and presages the darker passages in plays like *Macbeth* and *King Lear.* Critics have pointed out that in *Lucrece* Shakespeare shows evidence of trying "to realize the sensations of the two protagonists" in the same way that a dramatist must get inside the characters that he attempts to portray. In this sense, *Lucrece* is nearer to Shakespeare's dramatic creations than is *Venus and Adonis.* Some critics have found *Lucrece* more satisfactory than *Venus and Adonis* because it deals with realities rather than with "thin absurdities." Though the dramatic quality of *Lucrece* has won the praise of some, the majority have found the poem unsatisfactory. As Douglas Bush, in *Mythology and the Renaissance Tradition,* has commented, "Declamation roars while passion sleeps" and "Dramatic realism is likewise defeated by the incessant conceits."

"The Phoenix and the Turtle," a short poem slightly reminiscent of Chaucer's *Parlement of Foules,* was included, with Shakespeare's name appended, in a volume got together by Robert Chester under the title of *Love's Martyr, or, Rosalin's Complaint Allegorically Foreshadowing the Truth of Love* and published in a quarto version in 1601. Other contributors were John Marston, William Chapman, and Ben Jonson. Just why Shakespeare wrote a piece for this dull volume, no one knows. His brief contribution, however, reveals lyrical qualities of a high order. It inevitably reminds one of the songs that illuminate many of the plays, and we can forgive Chester for publishing so labored a work as *Love's Martyr* because he induced Shakespeare to write for it a lyric that ranks with the poet's finest songs. The work was republished in 1611, and Shakespeare's poem appeared for the third time in John Benson's edition of *Poems Written by Wil. Shakespeare* (1640). "The Phoenix and the Turtle" is now generally accepted as an authentic poem of Shakespeare's, though unlike anything else he ever wrote.

The poem is an elegy on the death of the phoenix, a mythological bird, and the turtledove, a symbol of faithfulness. The phoenix was believed to exist in Arabia where there was only one of its kind. At the end of its life span (500 years), it burned itself to death on a funeral pyre and from the ashes sprang a new phoenix.

In the conception of the poet, the birds have

HEREAFTER
FOLLOVV DIVERSE

Poeticall Essaies on the former Sub-
iect; viz: the *Turtle* and *Phœnix*.

*Done by the best and chiefest of our
moderne writers, with their names sub-
scribed to their particular workes:
neuer before extant.*

And (now first) consecrated by them all generally,
to the loue and merite of the true-noble Knight,
Sir Iohn Salisburie.

Dignum laude virum Musa vetat mori.

MDCI.

The title page of the *Turtle and Phoenix* supplement to Robert
Chester's *Love's Martyr* (1601).

been called to mourn the passing of the phoenix (here conceived of as a female bird) and the turtle-dove (a male bird) whose love was so great that they united as one in death as they mystically burned together. Some critics have seen in the poem an allegorical allusion to some contemporary love affair. One of the more absurd suggestions is that it refers to the love of Queen Elizabeth and the Earl of Essex; nothing could be further from historical truth. It is extremely doubtful that the poem has any profound allegorical significance of the kind that a few modern critics like to discover. Probably it merely symbolizes the union of beauty (the phoenix) and fidelity (the turtledove).

A volume of love poems entitled *The Passionate Pilgrim* was printed in 1599 by William Jaggard who attributed the authorship to William Shakespeare. Of its twenty poems, only five are generally conceded to be by Shakespeare. One of these is a version of Sonnet 138 which may derive from a copy earlier than that printed by Thorpe in the 1609 edition of Shakespeare's *Sonnets*. In choosing his title, Jaggard clearly intended to suggest a volume of amorous poems, for "passionate pilgrim" connoted to the Elizabethan an ardent lover. And in attributing the poems to Shakespeare, he was capitalizing upon a name that had already gained fame both as a narrative poet and as a playwright. In 1612, Thomas Heywood in *An Apology for Actors* appended a note condemning Jaggard for stealing some of his own poems, as well as Shakespeare's, and printing them in *The Passionate Pilgrim*. Heywood asserted that he knew that Shakespeare was "much offended with M.[aster] Jaggard (that altogether unknown to him) presumed to make so bold with his name."

"The Lover's Complaint" was appended to Thorpe's 1609 edition of the *Sonnets*. Its attribution to Shakespeare has been a matter of controversy, but critics recently have veered toward including it in the canon of the poet's works. At best it is a slight thing of no great value, but it is included here because of recent efforts to magnify its importance. The verse form is similar to that used in *Lucrece*, with faint resemblances to Edmund Spenser's diction and imagery. The story is that of a somewhat bedraggled maiden, seduced and abandoned by a lover so charming that she could not resist him. A shepherd comes upon her sitting beside a stream tearing up her love letters; to him she pours out her sorrowful tale.

During the later seventeenth and eighteenth centuries, Shakespeare's non-dramatic poems were neglected and almost forgotten. Shakespeare had staked his literary reputation upon these poems, and, as Leslie Stephens in *Studies of a Biographer* (1902) commented, he regarded his plays as "potboilers." Yet, ironically, during the second half of the seventeenth century the plays gained in popularity and the poems declined in the interest of the public. After the edition of *Venus and Adonis* in 1675, no separate edition appeared until 1866, and *Lucrece* did not have a separate edition after 1655 until 1768. The 1768 edition appeared without Shakespeare's name and with a changed title, *Tarquin and Lucrece, or, The Rape: A Poem*. Although the early editions remained available to some readers, and allusions to the poems are fairly frequent up to 1700, they rapidly fell into obscurity after that date.

Later readers and audiences found in Shakespeare's plays more satisfying poetry than the non-dramatic poems supplied. Even if Shakespeare himself did not dream that his plays would become fashionable—and enjoy immortality—he nevertheless lavished poetic imagination upon them, and the plays portray an infinitely more varied genius than one finds displayed in the non-dramatic poems. Yet these poems provide readers with a foretaste of the poetry in the plays, and they deserve the study of anyone concerned with the evolution of Shakespeare's poetic powers.

THE AUTHOR

As early as 1598 Shakespeare was so well known as a literary and dramatic craftsman that Francis Meres, in his *Palladis Tamia: Wits Treasury,* referred in flattering terms to him as "mellifluous and honey-tongued Shakespeare," famous for his *Venus and Adonis,* his *Lucrece,* and "his sugared sonnets," which were circulating "among his private friends." Meres observes further that "as Plautus and Seneca are accounted the best for comedy and tragedy among the Latins, so Shakespeare among the English is the most excellent in both kinds for the stage," and he mentions a dozen plays that had made a name for Shakespeare. He concludes with the remark that "the Muses would speak with

Shakespeare's fine filed phrase if they would speak English."

To those acquainted with the history of the Elizabethan and Jacobean periods, it is incredible that anyone should be so naïve or ignorant as to doubt the reality of Shakespeare as the author of the plays that bear his name. Yet so much nonsense has been written about other "candidates" for the plays that it is well to remind readers that no credible evidence that would stand up in a court of law has ever been adduced to prove either that Shakespeare did not write his plays or that anyone else wrote them. All the theories offered for the authorship of Francis Bacon, the Earl of Derby, the Earl of Oxford, the Earl of Hertford, Christopher Marlowe, and a score of other candidates are mere conjectures spun from the active imaginations of persons who confuse hypothesis and conjecture with evidence.

As Meres' statement of 1598 indicates, Shakespeare was already a popular playwright whose name carried weight at the box office. The obvious reputation of Shakespeare as early as 1598 makes the effort to prove him a myth one of the most absurd in the history of human perversity.

The anti-Shakespeareans talk darkly about a plot of vested interests to maintain the authorship of Shakespeare. Nobody has any vested interest in Shakespeare, but every scholar is interested in the truth and in the quality of evidence advanced by special pleaders who set forth hypotheses in place of facts.

The anti-Shakespeareans base their arguments

upon a few simple premises, all of them false. These false premises are that Shakespeare was an unlettered yokel without any schooling, that nothing is known about Shakespeare, and that only a noble lord or the equivalent in background could have written the plays. The facts are that more is known about Shakespeare than about most dramatists of his day, that he had a very good education, acquired in the Stratford Grammar School, that the plays show no evidence of profound book learning, and that the knowledge of kings and courts evident in the plays is no greater than any intelligent young man could have picked up at second hand. Most anti-Shakespeareans are naïve and betray an obvious snobbery. The author of their favorite plays, they imply, must have had a college diploma framed and hung on his study wall like the one in their dentist's office, and obviously so great a writer must have had a title or some equally significant evidence of exalted social background. They forget that genius has a way of cropping up in unexpected places and that none of the great creative writers of the world got his inspiration in a college or university course.

William Shakespeare was the son of John Shakespeare of Stratford-upon-Avon, a substantial citizen of that small but busy market town in the center of the rich agricultural county of Warwick. John Shakespeare kept a shop, what we would call a general store; he dealt in wool and other produce and gradually acquired property. As a youth, John Shakespeare had learned the trade of glover and leather worker. There is no contemporary evidence that the elder Shakespeare was a butcher, though the anti-Shakespeareans like to talk about the ignorant "butcher's boy of Stratford." Their only evidence is a statement by gossipy John Aubrey, more than a century after William Shakespeare's birth, that young William followed his father's trade, and when he killed a calf, "he would do it in a high style and make a speech." We would like to believe the story true, but Aubrey is not a very credible witness.

John Shakespeare probably continued to operate a farm at Snitterfield that his father had leased. He married Mary Arden, daughter of his father's landlord, a man of some property. The third of their eight children was William, baptized on April 26, 1564, and probably born three days before. At least, it is conventional to celebrate April 23 as his birthday.

The Stratford records give considerable information about John Shakespeare. We know that he held several municipal offices including those of alderman and mayor. In 1580 he was in some sort of legal difficulty and was fined for neglecting a summons of the Court of Queen's Bench requiring him to appear at Westminster and be bound over to keep the peace.

As a citizen and alderman of Stratford, John Shakespeare was entitled to send his son to the grammar school free. Though the records are lost, there can be no reason to doubt that this is where young William received his education. As any student of the period knows, the grammar schools provided the basic education in Latin learning and literature. The Elizabethan grammar school is not to be confused with modern grammar schools. Many cultivated men of the day received all their formal education in the grammar schools. At the universities in this period a student would have received little training that would have inspired him to be a creative writer. At Stratford young Shakespeare would have acquired a familiarity with Latin and some little knowledge of Greek. He would have read Latin authors and become acquainted with the plays of Plautus and Terence. Undoubtedly, in this period of his life he received that stimulation to read and explore for himself the world of ancient and modern history which he later utilized in his plays. The youngster who does not acquire this type of intellectual curiosity *before* college days rarely develops as a result of a college course the kind of mind Shakespeare demonstrated. His learning in books was anything but profound, but he clearly had the probing curiosity that sent him in search of information, and he had a keenness in the observation of nature and of humankind that finds reflection in his poetry.

There is little documentation for Shakespeare's boyhood. There is little reason why there should be. Nobody knew that he was going to be a dramatist about whom any scrap of information would be prized in the centuries to come. He was merely an active and vigorous youth of Stratford, perhaps assisting his father in his business, and no Boswell bothered to write down facts about him. The most important record that we have is a marriage license issued by the Bishop of Worcester on November

27, 1582, to permit William Shakespeare to marry Anne Hathaway, seven or eight years his senior; furthermore, the Bishop permitted the marriage after reading the banns only once instead of three times, evidence of the desire for haste. The need was explained on May 26, 1583, when the christening of Susanna, daughter of William and Anne Shakespeare, was recorded at Stratford. Two years later, on February 2, 1585, the records show the birth of twins to the Shakespeares, a boy and a girl who were christened Hamnet and Judith.

What William Shakespeare was doing in Stratford during the early years of his married life, or when he went to London, we do not know. It has been conjectured that he tried his hand at schoolteaching, but that is a mere guess. There is a legend that he left Stratford to escape a charge of poaching in the park of Sir Thomas Lucy of Charlecote, but there is no proof of this. There is also a legend that when first he came to London he earned his living by holding horses outside a playhouse and presently was given employment inside, but there is nothing better than eighteenth-century hearsay for this. How Shakespeare broke into the London theatres as a dramatist and actor we do not know. But lack of information is not surprising, for Elizabethans did not write their autobiographies, and we know even less about the lives of many writers and some men of affairs than we know about Shakespeare. By 1592 he was so well established and popular that he incurred the envy of the dramatist and pamphleteer Robert Greene, who referred to him as an "upstart crow . . . in his own conceit the only Shake-scene in a country." From this time onward, contemporary allusions and references in legal documents enable the scholar to chart Shakespeare's career with greater accuracy than is possible with most other Elizabethan dramatists.

By 1594 Shakespeare was a member of the company of actors known as the Lord Chamberlain's Men. After the accession of James I, in 1603, the company would have the sovereign for their patron and would be known as the King's Men. During the period of its greatest prosperity, this company would have as its principal theatres the Globe and the Blackfriars. Shakespeare was both an actor and a shareholder in the company. Tradition has assigned him such acting roles as Adam in *As You Like It* and the Ghost in *Hamlet,* a modest place on the stage that suggests that he may have had other duties in the management of the company. Such conclusions, however, are based on surmise.

What we do know is that his plays were popular and that he was highly successful in his vocation. His first play may have been *The Comedy of Errors,* acted perhaps in 1591. Certainly this was one of his earliest plays. The three parts of *Henry VI* were acted sometime between 1590 and 1592. Critics are not in agreement about precisely how much Shakespeare wrote of these three plays. *Richard III* probably dates from 1593. With this play Shakespeare captured the imagination of Elizabethan audiences, then enormously interested in historical plays. With *Richard III* Shakespeare also gave an interpretation pleasing to the Tudors of the rise to power of the grandfather of Queen Elizabeth. From this time onward, Shakespeare's plays followed on the stage in rapid succession: *Titus Andronicus, The Taming of the Shrew, The Two Gentlemen of Verona, Love's Labor's Lost, Romeo and Juliet, Richard II, A Midsummer Night's Dream, King John, The Merchant of Venice, Henry IV (Parts 1 and 2), Much Ado about Nothing, Henry V, Julius Cæsar, As You Like It, Twelfth Night, Hamlet, The Merry Wives of Windsor, All's Well That Ends Well, Measure for Measure, Othello, King Lear,* and nine others that followed before Shakespeare retired completely, about 1613.

In the course of his career in London, he made enough money to enable him to retire to Stratford with a competence. His purchase on May 4, 1597, of New Place, then the second-largest dwelling in Stratford, "a pretty house of brick and timber," with a handsome garden, indicates his increasing prosperity. There his wife and children lived while he busied himself in the London theatres. The summer before he acquired New Place, his life was darkened by the death of his only son, Hamnet, a child of eleven. In May, 1602, Shakespeare purchased one hundred and seven acres of fertile farmland near Stratford and a few months later bought a cottage and garden across the alley from New Place. About 1611, he seems to have returned permanently to Stratford, for the next year a legal document refers to him as "William Shakespeare of Stratford-upon-Avon . . . gentleman." To achieve the desired appellation of gentleman, William Shakespeare had seen to it that the College of Heralds in 1596 granted his father a coat of arms. In one step he thus became a second-generation gentleman.

Shakespeare's daughter Susanna made a good match in 1607 with Dr. John Hall, a prominent and prosperous Stratford physician. His second daughter, Judith, did not marry until she was thirty-one years old, and then, under somewhat scandalous circumstances, she married Thomas Quiney, a Stratford vintner. On March 25, 1616, Shakespeare made his will, bequeathing his landed property to Susanna, £300 to Judith, certain sums to other relatives, and his second-best bed to his wife, Anne. Much has been made of the second-best bed, but the legacy probably indicates only that Anne liked that particular bed. Shakespeare, following the practice of the time, may have already arranged with Susanna for his wife's care. Finally, on April 23, 1616, the anniversary of his birth, William Shakespeare died, and he was buried on April 25 within the chancel of Trinity Church, as befitted an honored citizen. On August 6, 1623, a few months before the publication of the collected edition of Shakespeare's plays, Anne Shakespeare joined her husband in death.

THE PUBLICATION OF HIS PLAYS

During his lifetime Shakespeare made no effort to publish any of his plays, though eighteen appeared in print in single-play editions known as quartos. Some of these are corrupt versions known as "bad quartos." No quarto, so far as is known, had the author's approval. Plays were not considered "lit-

erature" any more than most radio and television
scripts today are considered literature. Dramatists
sold their plays outright to the theatrical companies
and it was usually considered in the company's interest to keep plays from getting into print. To
achieve a reputation as a man of letters, Shakespeare wrote his *Sonnets* and his narrative poems,
Venus and Adonis and *The Rape of Lucrece,* but
he probably never dreamed that his plays would
establish his reputation as a literary genius. Only
Ben Jonson, a man known for his colossal conceit,
had the crust to call his plays *Works,* as he did
when he published an edition in 1616. But men
laughed at Ben Jonson.

After Shakespeare's death, two of his old colleagues in the King's Men, John Heminges and
Henry Condell, decided that it would be a good
thing to print, in more accurate versions than were
then available, the plays already published and
eighteen additional plays not previously published
in quarto. In 1623 appeared *Mr. William Shakespeares Comedies, Histories, & Tragedies. Published according to the True Originall Copies.
London. Printed by Isaac Iaggard and Ed. Blount.*
This was the famous First Folio, a work that had the
authority of Shakespeare's associates. The only play
commonly attributed to Shakespeare that was omit-
ted in the First Folio was *Pericles.* In their preface,
"To the great Variety of Readers," Heminges and
Condell state that whereas "you were abused with
diverse stolen and surreptitious copies, maimed and
deformed by the frauds and stealths of injurious
impostors that exposed them, even those are now

offered to your view cured and perfect of their limbs; and all the rest, absolute in their numbers, as he conceived them." What they used for printer's copy is one of the vexed problems of scholarship, and skilled bibliographers have devoted years of study to the question of the relation of the "copy" for the First Folio to Shakespeare's manuscripts. In some cases it is clear that the editors corrected printed quarto versions of the plays, probably by comparison with playhouse scripts. Whether these scripts were in Shakespeare's autograph is anybody's guess. No manuscript of any play in Shakespeare's handwriting has survived. Indeed, very few play manuscripts from this period by any author are extant. The Tudor and Stuart periods had not yet learned to prize autographs and authors' original manuscripts.

Since the First Folio contains eighteen plays not previously printed, it is the only source for these. For the other eighteen, which had appeared in quarto versions, the First Folio also has the authority of an edition prepared and overseen by Shakespeare's colleagues and professional associates. But since editorial standards in 1623 were far from strict, and Heminges and Condell were actors rather than editors by profession, the texts are sometimes careless. The printing and proofreading of the First Folio also left much to be desired, and some garbled passages have had to be corrected and emended. The "good quarto" texts have to be taken into account in preparing a modern edition.

Because of the great popularity of Shakespeare through the centuries, the First Folio has become a prized book, but it is not a very rare one, for it is estimated that 238 copies are extant. The Folger Shakespeare Library in Washington, D.C., has seventy-nine copies of the First Folio, collected by the founder, Henry Clay Folger, who believed that a collation of as many texts as possible would reveal significant facts about the text of Shakespeare's plays. Dr. Charlton Hinman, using an ingenious machine of his own invention for mechanical collating, has made many discoveries that throw light on Shakespeare's text and on printing practices of the day.

The probability is that the First Folio of 1623 had an edition of between 1,000 and 1,250 copies. It is believed that it sold for £1, which made it an expensive book, for £1 in 1623 was equivalent to something between $40 and $50 in modern purchasing power.

During the seventeenth century, Shakespeare was sufficiently popular to warrant three later editions in folio size, the Second Folio of 1632, the Third Folio of 1663–1664, and the Fourth Folio of 1685. The Third Folio added six other plays ascribed to Shakespeare, but these are apocryphal.

THE SHAKESPEAREAN THEATRE

The theatres in which Shakespeare's plays were performed were vastly different from those we know today. The stage was a platform that jutted out into the area now occupied by the first rows of seats on the main floor, what is called the "orchestra" in America and the "pit" in England. This platform had no curtain to come down at the ends of acts and scenes. And although simple stage properties were available, the Elizabethan theatre lacked both the machinery and the elaborate movable scenery of the modern theatre. In the rear of the platform stage was a curtained area that could be used as an inner room, a tomb, or any such scene that might be required. A balcony above this inner room, and perhaps balconies on the sides of the stage, could represent the upper deck of a ship, the entry to Juliet's room, or a prison window. A trap door in the stage provided an entrance for ghosts and devils from the nether regions, and a similar trap in the canopied structure over the stage, known as the "heavens," made it possible to let down angels on a rope. These primitive stage arrangements help to account for many elements in Elizabethan plays. For example, since there was no curtain, the dramatist frequently felt the necessity of writing into his play action to clear the stage at the ends of acts and scenes. The funeral march at the end of *Hamlet* is not there merely for atmosphere; Shakespeare had to get the corpses off the stage. The lack of scenery also freed the dramatist from undue concern about the exact location of his sets, and the physical relation of his various settings to each other did not have to be worked out with the same precision as in the modern theatre.

Before London had buildings designed exclusively for theatrical entertainment, plays were given in inns and taverns. The characteristic inn of the period had an inner courtyard with rooms opening onto balconies overlooking the yard. Players could set up their temporary stages at one end of the yard and audiences could find seats on the balconies out of the weather. The poorer sort could stand or sit on the cobblestones in the yard, which was open to the sky. The first theatres followed this construction, and throughout the Elizabethan period the large public theatres had a yard in front of the stage open to the weather, with two or three tiers of covered balconies extending around the theatre. This physical structure again influenced the writing of plays. Because a dramatist wanted the actors to be heard, he frequently wrote into his play orations that could be delivered with declamatory effect. He also provided spectacle, buffoonery, and broad jests to keep the riotous groundlings in the yard entertained and quiet.

In another respect the Elizabethan theatre differed greatly from ours. It had no actresses. All women's roles were taken by boys, sometimes recruited from the boys' choirs of the London churches. Some of these youths acted their roles with great skill and the Elizabethans did not seem to be aware of any incongruity. The first actresses on the professional English stage appeared after the Restoration of Charles II, in 1660, when exiled Englishmen brought back from France practices of the French stage.

London in the Elizabethan period, as now, was the center of theatrical interest, though wandering actors from time to time traveled through the country performing in inns, halls, and the houses of the nobility. The first professional playhouse, called simply The Theatre, was erected by James Burbage, father of Shakespeare's colleague Richard Burbage, in 1576 on lands of the old Holywell Priory adjacent to Finsbury Fields, a playground and park area just north of the city walls. It had the advantage of being outside the city's jurisdiction and yet was near enough to be easily accessible. Soon after The Theatre was opened, another playhouse called The Curtain was erected in the same neighborhood. Both of these playhouses had open courtyards and were probably polygonal in shape.

About the time The Curtain opened, Richard Farrant, Master of the Children of the Chapel Royal at Windsor and of St. Paul's, conceived the idea of opening a "private" theatre in the old monastery buildings of the Blackfriars, not far from St. Paul's Cathedral in the heart of the city. This theatre was ostensibly to train the choirboys in plays for presentation at Court, but Farrant managed to present plays to paying audiences and achieved considerable success until aristocratic neighbors complained and had the theatre closed. The first Blackfriars Theatre was significant, however, because it popularized the boy actors in a professional way and it paved the way for a second theatre in the Blackfriars, which Shakespeare's company took over more than thirty years later. By the last years of the sixteenth century, London had at least six professional theatres and still others were erected during the reign of James I.

The Globe Theatre, the playhouse that most people connect with Shakespeare, was erected early in 1599 on the Bankside, the area across the Thames from the city. Its construction had a dramatic beginning, for on the night of December 28, 1598, James Burbage's sons, Cuthbert and Richard, gathered together a crew who tore down the old theatre in Holywell and carted the timbers across the river to a site they had chosen for a new playhouse. The reason for this clandestine operation was a row with the landowner over the lease to the Holywell property. The site chosen for the Globe was another playground outside of the city's jurisdiction, a region of somewhat unsavory character. Not far away was the Bear Garden, an amphitheatre devoted to the baiting of bears and bulls. This was also the region occupied by many houses of ill fame licensed by the Bishop of Winchester and the source of substantial revenue to him. But it was easily accessible either from London Bridge or by means of the cheap boats operated by the London watermen, and it had the great advantage of being beyond the authority of the Puritanical aldermen of London, who frowned on plays because they lured apprentices from work, filled their heads with improper ideas, and generally exerted a bad influence. The aldermen also complained that the crowds drawn together in the theatre helped to spread the plague.

The Globe was the handsomest theatre up to its time. It was a large building, apparently octagonal in shape, and open like its predecessors to the sky in the center, but capable of seating a large audience in its covered balconies. To erect and operate the Globe, the Burbages organized a syndicate composed of the leading members of the dramatic company, of which Shakespeare was a member.

Since it was open to the weather and depended on natural light, plays had to be given in the afternoon. This caused no hardship in the long afternoons of an English summer, but in the winter the weather was a great handicap and discouraged all except the hardiest. For that reason, in 1608 Shakespeare's company was glad to take over the lease of the second Blackfriars Theatre, a substantial, roomy hall reconstructed within the framework of the old monastery building. This theatre was protected from the weather and its stage was artificially lighted by chandeliers of candles. This became the winter playhouse for Shakespeare's company and at once proved so popular that the congestion of traffic created an embarrassing problem. Stringent regulations had to be made for the movement of coaches in the vicinity. Shakespeare's company continued to use the Globe during the summer months. In 1613 a squib fired from a cannon during a performance of *Henry VIII* fell on the thatched roof and the Globe burned to the ground. The next year it was rebuilt.

London had other famous theatres. The Rose, just west of the Globe, was built by Philip Henslowe, a semiliterate denizen of the Bankside, who became one of the most important theatrical owners and producers of the Tudor and Stuart periods. What is more important for historians, he kept a detailed account book, which provides much of our information about theatrical history in his time. Another famous theatre on the Bankside was the Swan, which a Dutch priest, Johannes de Witt, visited in 1596. The crude drawing of the stage which he made was copied by his friend Arend van Buchell; it is one of the important pieces of contemporary evidence for theatrical construction. Among the other theatres, the Fortune, north of the city, on Golding Lane, and the Red Bull, even farther away from the city, off St. John's Street, were the most popular. The Red Bull, much frequented by apprentices, favored sensational and sometimes rowdy plays.

The actors who kept all of these theatres going were organized into companies under the protection of some noble patron. Traditionally actors had enjoyed a low reputation. In some of the ordinances they were classed as vagrants; in the phraseology of the time, "rogues, vagabonds, sturdy beggars, and common players" were all listed together as undesirables. To escape penalties often meted out to these characters, organized groups of actors managed to gain the protection of various personages of high degree. In the later years of Elizabeth's reign, a group flourished under the name of the Queen's Men; another group had the protection of the Lord Admiral and were known as the Lord Admiral's Men. Edward Alleyn, son-in-law of Philip Henslowe, was the leading spirit in the Lord Admiral's Men. Besides the adult companies, troupes of boy actors from time to time also enjoyed considerable popularity. Among these were the Children of Paul's and the Children of the Chapel Royal.

The company with which Shakespeare had a long association had for its first patron Henry Carey, Lord Hunsdon, the Lord Chamberlain, and hence they were known as the Lord Chamberlain's Men. After the accession of James I, they became the

King's Men. This company was the great rival of the Lord Admiral's Men, managed by Henslowe and Alleyn.

All was not easy for the players in Shakespeare's time, for the aldermen of London were always eager for an excuse to close up the Blackfriars and any other theatres in their jurisdiction. The theatres outside the jurisdiction of London were not immune from interference, for they might be shut up by order of the Privy Council for meddling in politics or for various other offenses, or they might be closed in time of plague lest they spread infection. During plague times, the actors usually went on tour and played the provinces wherever they could find an audience. Particularly frightening were the plagues of 1592–1594 and 1613 when the theatres closed and the players, like many other Londoners, had to take to the country.

Though players had a low social status, they enjoyed great popularity, and one of the favorite forms of entertainment at Court was the performance of plays. To be commanded to perform at Court conferred great prestige upon a company of players, and printers frequently noted that fact when they published plays. Several of Shakespeare's plays were performed before the sovereign, and Shakespeare himself undoubtedly acted in some of these plays.

REFERENCES FOR FURTHER READING

Many readers will want suggestions for further reading about Shakespeare and his times. A few references will serve as guides to further study in the enormous literature on the subject. A simple and useful little book is Gerald Sanders, *A Shakespeare Primer* (New York, 1950). *A Companion to Shakespeare Studies,* edited by Harley Granville-Barker and G. B. Harrison (Cambridge, 1934), is a valuable guide. A concise handbook of facts about Shakespeare is Gerald E. Bentley, *Shakespeare: A Biographical Handbook* (New Haven, 1961). More detailed but not so voluminous as to be confusing is Hazelton Spencer, *The Art and Life of William Shakespeare* (New York, 1940), which, like Sanders' and Bentley's handbooks, contains a brief annotated list of useful books on various aspects of the subject. The most detailed and scholarly work providing complete factual information about Shakespeare is Sir Edmund Chambers, *William Shakespeare: A Study of Facts and Problems* (2 vols., Oxford, 1930).

Among other biographies of Shakespeare, Joseph Quincy Adams, *A Life of William Shakespeare* (Boston, 1923) is still an excellent assessment of the essential facts and the traditional information, and Marchette Chute, *Shakespeare of London* (New York, 1949; paperback, 1957) stresses Shakespeare's life in the theatre. Two new biographies of Shakespeare have recently appeared. A. L. Rowse, *William Shakespeare: A Biography* (London, 1963; New York, 1964) provides an appraisal by an English historian, who dismisses the notion that somebody else wrote Shakespeare's plays as arrant nonsense that runs counter to known historical fact. Peter Quennell, *Shakespeare: A Biography* (Cleveland and New York, 1963) is a sensitive and intelligent survey of what is known and surmised of Shakespeare's life. Louis B. Wright, *Shakespeare for Everyman* (New York, 1964; 1965) discusses the basis of Shakespeare's enduring popularity.

The *Shakespeare Quarterly*, published by the Shakespeare Association of America under the editorship of James G. McManaway, is recommended for those who wish to keep up with current Shakespearean scholarship and stage productions. The *Quarterly* includes an annual bibliography of Shakespeare editions and works on Shakespeare published during the previous year.

The question of the authenticity of Shakespeare's plays arouses perennial attention. The theory of hidden cryptograms in the plays is demolished by William F. and Elizebeth S. Friedman, *The Shakespearean Ciphers Examined* (New York, 1957). A succinct account of the various absurdities advanced to suggest the authorship of a multitude of candidates other than Shakespeare will be found in R. C. Churchill, *Shakespeare and His Betters* (Bloomington, Ind., 1959). Another recent discussion of the subject, *The Authorship of Shakespeare*, by James G. McManaway (Washington, D.C., 1962), presents the evidence from contemporary records to prove the identity of Shakespeare the actor-playwright with Shakespeare of Stratford. A careful analysis of recent contentions about the authorship problem, and a dismissal of the conjectures, especially those of the Oxfordians, will be found in Milward W. Martin, *Was Shakespeare Shakespeare? A Lawyer Reviews the Evidence* (New York, 1965).

Scholars are not in agreement about the details

of playhouse construction in the Elizabethan period. John C. Adams presents a plausible reconstruction of the Globe in *The Globe Playhouse: Its Design and Equipment* (Cambridge, Mass., 1942; 2nd rev. ed., 1961). A description with excellent drawings based on Dr. Adams' model is Irwin Smith, *Shakespeare's Globe Playhouse: A Modern Reconstruction in Text and Scale Drawings* (New York, 1956). Other sensible discussions are W. Walter Hodges, *The Globe Restored* (London, 1953) and A. M. Nagler, *Shakespeare's Stage* (New Haven, 1958). Bernard Beckerman, *Shakespeare at the Globe, 1599–1609* (New Haven, 1962; paperback, 1962) discusses Elizabethan staging and acting techniques.

A sound and readable history of the early theatres is Joseph Quincy Adams, *Shakespearean Playhouses: A History of English Theatres from the Beginnings to the Restoration* (Boston, 1917). For detailed, factual information about the Elizabethan and seventeenth-century stages, the definitive reference works are Sir Edmund Chambers, *The Elizabethan Stage* (4 vols., Oxford, 1923) and Gerald E. Bentley, *The Jacobean and Caroline Stages* (5 vols., Oxford, 1941–1956).

Further information on the history of the theatre and related topics will be found in the following titles: T. W. Baldwin, *The Organization and Personnel of the Shakespearean Company* (Princeton, 1927); Lily Bess Campbell, *Scenes and Machines on the English Stage during the Renaissance* (Cambridge, 1923); Esther Cloudman Dunn, *Shakespeare in America* (New York, 1939); George C. D. Odell, *Shakespeare from Betterton to Irving* (2 vols., London, 1931); Arthur Colby Sprague, *Shakespeare and the Actors: The Stage Business in His Plays (1660–1905)* (Cambridge, Mass., 1944) and *Shakespearian Players and Performances* (Cambridge, Mass., 1953); Leslie Hotson, *The Commonwealth and Restoration Stage* (Cambridge, Mass., 1928); Alwin Thaler, *Shakspere to Sheridan: A Book about the Theatre of Yesterday and To-day* (Cambridge, Mass., 1922); George C. Branam, *Eighteenth-Century Adaptations of Shakespeare's Tragedies* (Berkeley, 1956); C. Beecher Hogan, *Shakespeare in the Theatre, 1701–1800* (Oxford, 1957); Ernest Bradlee Watson, *Sheridan to Robertson: A Study of the 19th-Century London Stage* (Cambridge, Mass., 1926); and Enid Welsford, *The Court Masque* (Cambridge, Mass., 1927).

A brief account of the growth of Shakespeare's reputation is F. E. Halliday, *The Cult of Shakespeare* (London, 1947). A more detailed discussion is given in Augustus Ralli, *A History of Shakespearian Criticism* (2 vols., Oxford, 1932; New York, 1958). Harley Granville-Barker, *Prefaces to Shakespeare* (5 vols., London, 1927–1948; 2 vols., London, 1958) provides stimulating critical discussion of the plays. An older classic of criticism is Andrew C. Bradley, *Shakespearean Tragedy: Lectures on Hamlet, Othello, King Lear, Macbeth* (London, 1904; paperback, 1955). Sir Edmund Chambers, *Shakespeare: A Survey* (London, 1935; paperback, 1958) contains short, sensible essays on thirty-four of the plays, originally written as introductions to single-play editions. Alfred Harbage, *William Shakespeare: A Reader's Guide* (New York, 1963) is a handbook to the reading and appreciation of the plays, with scene synopses and interpretation.

For the history plays see Lily Bess Campbell, *Shakespeare's "Histories": Mirrors of Elizabethan Policy* (Cambridge, 1947); John Palmer, *Political Characters of Shakespeare* (London, 1945; 1961); E. M. W. Tillyard, *Shakespeare's History Plays* (London, 1948); Irving Ribner, *The English History Play in the Age of Shakespeare* (Princeton, 1947; rev. ed., New York, 1965); Max M. Reese, *The Cease of Majesty* (London, 1961); and Arthur Colby Sprague, *Shakespeare's Histories: Plays for the Stage* (London, 1964). Harold Jenkins, "Shakespeare's History Plays: 1900–1951," *Shakespeare Survey 6* (Cambridge, 1953), 1–15, provides an excellent survey of recent critical opinion on the subject.

An extraordinary summary of the scholarship and criticism of Shakespeare's poems will be found in Hyder E. Rollins, *A New Variorum Edition of Shakespeare: The Poems* (Philadelphia, 1938). A briefer but excellent summary will be found in F. T. Prince, *The Arden Edition of the Works of William Shakespeare: The Poems* (London, 1960). Prince's introduction is succinct, clear, and sensible. The New Cambridge edition of *The Poems* (Cambridge, 1966), edited by J. C. Maxwell, also has a useful and perspicacious introduction that takes into account recent scholarly opinion. Hallett Smith, *Elizabethan Poetry: A Study in Conventions, Meaning, and Expression* (Cambridge, Mass., 1953), provides an excellent chapter on Shakespeare's place among the Ovidian poets. Douglas Bush, *Mythology and the Renaissance Tradition in English Poetry* (Minneapolis, 1932; revised edition, 1963), also has valuable sidelights on Shakespeare's *Poems*. A review of current scholarship on the *Poems* will be found in *Shakespeare Survey 15*, edited by Allardyce Nicoll, (Cambridge, 1962). A mass of information on the subject is included in T. W. Baldwin, *On the Literary Genetics of Shakespere's Poems and Sonnets* (Urbana, Ill., 1950). For recent comment on "The Phoenix and the Turtle," see William H. Matchett, *The Phoenix and the Turtle* (The Hague, 1965).

The comedies are illuminated by the following studies: C. L. Barber, *Shakespeare's Festive Comedy* (Princeton, 1959); John Russell Brown, *Shakespeare and His Comedies* (London, 1957); H. B. Charlton, *Shakespearian Comedy* (London, 1938; 4th ed., 1949); W. W. Lawrence, *Shakespeare's Problem Comedies* (New York, 1931); and Thomas M. Parrott, *Shakespearean Comedy* (New York, 1949).

Further discussions of Shakespeare's tragedies, in addition to Bradley, already cited, are contained in H. B. Charlton, *Shakespearian Tragedy* (Cambridge, 1948); Willard Farnham, *The Medieval Heritage of Elizabethan Tragedy* (Berkeley, 1936) and *Shakespeare's Tragic Frontier: The World of His Final Tragedies* (Berkeley, 1950); and Harold S. Wilson, *On the Design of Shakespearian Tragedy* (Toronto, 1957).

Kenneth Muir, *Shakespeare's Sources: Comedies and Tragedies* (London, 1957) discusses Shakespeare's use of source material. The sources themselves have been reprinted several times. Among old editions are John P. Collier (ed.), *Shakespeare's*

Library (2 vols., London, 1850), Israel C. Gollancz (ed.), *The Shakespeare Classics* (12 vols., London, 1907–1926), and W. C. Hazlitt (ed.), *Shakespeare's Library* (6 vols., London, 1875). A modern edition is being prepared by Geoffrey Bullough with the title *Narrative and Dramatic Sources of Shakespeare* (London and New York, 1957–). Six volumes, covering the sources for all the plays except the tragedies, have been published to date (1967).

In addition to the second edition of *Webster's New International Dictionary,* which contains most of the unusual words used by Shakespeare, the following reference works are helpful: Edwin A. Abbott, *A Shakespearian Grammar* (London, 1872; reprinted in paperback, 1966); C. T. Onions, *A Shakespeare Glossary* (2nd rev. ed., Oxford, 1925); and Eric Partridge, *Shakespeare's Bawdy* (New York, 1948; paperback, 1960).

Some knowledge of the social background of the period in which Shakespeare lived is important for a full understanding of his work. A brief, clear, and accurate account of Tudor history is S. T. Bindoff, *The Tudors,* in the Penguin series. A readable general history is G. M. Trevelyan, *The History of England,* first published in 1926 and available in numerous editions. The same author's *English Social History,* first published in 1942 and also available in many editions, provides fascinating information about England in all periods. Sir John Neale, *Queen Elizabeth* (London, 1935; paperback, 1957) is the best study of the great Queen. Various aspects of life in the Elizabethan period are treated in Louis B. Wright, *Middle-class Culture in Elizabethan*

England (Chapel Hill, N.C., 1935; reprinted Ithaca, N.Y., 1958, 1964). *Shakespeare's England: An Account of the Life and Manners of His Age,* edited by Sidney Lee and C. T. Onions (2 vols., Oxford, 1917), provides much information on many aspects of Elizabethan life. A fascinating survey of the period will be found in Muriel St. C. Byrne, *Elizabethan Life in Town and Country* (London, 1925; rev. ed., 1954; paperback, 1961). An informative and useful little book is James Sutherland and Joel Hurstfield, *Shakespeare's World* (London, 1964). A great deal of concise and useful information will be found in *The Reader's Encyclopedia of Shakespeare,* compiled by Oscar J. Campbell and Edward G. Quinn (New York, 1966).

The Folger Library is issuing a series of illustrated booklets entitled "Folger Booklets on Tudor and Stuart Civilization," printed and distributed by The University Press of Virginia, Charlottesville, Va. Published to date are the following titles:

D. W. Davies, *Dutch Influences on English Culture, 1558–1625*

Giles E. Dawson, *The Life of William Shakespeare*

Ellen C. Eyler, *Early English Gardens and Garden Books*

Elaine W. Fowler, *English Sea Power in the Early Tudor Period, 1485–1558*

John R. Hale, *The Art of War and Renaissance England*

William Haller, *Elizabeth I and the Puritans*

F. D. and J. F. M. Hoeniger, *The Development of Natural History in Tudor England*

———, *The Growth of Natural History in Stuart England: From Gerard to the Royal Society*

Virginia A. LaMar, *English Dress in the Age of Shakespeare*

———, *Travel and Roads in England*

John L. Lievsay, *The Elizabethan Image of Italy*

James G. McManaway, *The Authorship of Shakespeare*

Dorothy E. Mason, *Music in Elizabethan England*

Garrett Mattingly, *The "Invincible" Armada and Elizabethan England*

Boies Penrose, *Tudor and Early Stuart Voyaging*

T. I. Rae, *Scotland in the Time of Shakespeare*

Conyers Read, *The Government of England under Elizabeth*

Albert J. Schmidt, *The Yeoman in Tudor and Stuart England*

Lilly C. Stone, *English Sports and Recreations*

Craig R. Thompson, *The Bible in English, 1525–1611*

———, *The English Church in the Sixteenth Century*

———, *Schools in Tudor England*

———, *Universities in Tudor England*

Louis B. Wright, *Shakespeare's Theatre and the Dramatic Tradition*

At intervals the Folger Library plans to gather these booklets in hardbound volumes. The first is *Life and Letters in Tudor and Stuart England, First Folger Series,* edited by Louis B. Wright and Virginia A. LaMar (now being distributed by The University Press of Virginia). The volume contains eleven of the separate booklets.

SHAKESPEARE'S POEMS

The Latin quotation is from Ovid's *Amores*, I, xv, 35-36: "Let cheap things excite the multitude; for me, may golden Apollo serve full cups from the Castalian spring." Ben Jonson gave a free translation of these lines: "Kneel hinds to trash: me let bright Phoebus swell, / With cups full flowing from the Muses' well [the Castalian spring]."

VENUS AND ADONIS

*Vilia miretur vulgus; mihi flavus Apollo
Pocula Castalia plena ministret aqua*

Henry Wriothesley (pronounced *risley*), third Earl of Southampton, was born on October 6, 1573, which would have made him under twenty when Shakespeare wrote his dedication. The tone suggests that Shakespeare was not yet well acquainted with the nobleman.

||||||||||||||||||||||||||||||||||||||

first heir of my invention: probably meaning, first literary effort, since plays were not considered literature.

ear: plant.

TO THE

RIGHT HONORABLE
HENRY WRIOTHESLEY,

EARL OF SOUTHAMPTON, AND BARON
OF TITCHFIELD

RIGHT HONORABLE,

I know not how I shall offend in dedicating my unpolished lines to your lordship, nor how the world will censure me for choosing so strong a prop to support so weak a burden: only, if your honor seem but pleased, I account myself highly praised, and vow to take advantage of all idle hours, till I have honored you with some graver labor. But if the first heir of my invention prove deformed, I shall be sorry it had so noble a godfather, and never after ear so barren a land, for fear it yield me still so bad a harvest. I leave it to your honorable survey, and your honor to your heart's content; which I wish may always answer your own wish, and the world's hopeful expectation.

Your honor's in all duty,
William Shakespeare

The verse form of *Venus and Adonis*, a six-line stanza rhyming *ab ab cc*, was popular at this time. Thomas Lodge's erotic poem, *Scilla's Metamorphosis* (1589), was written in this verse form, as were other contemporary poems.

▪▪▪▪▪▪▪▪▪▪▪▪▪▪▪▪▪▪▪▪▪▪▪▪▪▪▪▪▪▪

1. **purple-colored:** bright colored.
2. **weeping:** dew covered.
5. **makes amain:** hurries.
9. **Stain to all nymphs:** your beauty makes all nymphs look tarnished.
11. **Nature . . . strife:** Nature outdid herself.
13. **Vouchsafe:** consent.
15. **meed:** reward.
18. **set:** seated.

Hunters setting out for the chase. From George Turberville, *The Noble Art of Venery* (ca. 1576).

VENUS AND ADONIS

EVEN as the sun with purple-colored face
Had ta'en his last leave of the weeping morn,
Rose-cheeked Adonis hied him to the chase;
Hunting he loved, but love he laughed to scorn.
　　Sick-thoughted Venus makes amain unto him,　　5
　　And like a bold-faced suitor 'gins to woo him.

"Thrice fairer than myself," thus she began,
"The field's chief flower, sweet above compare,
Stain to all nymphs, more lovely than a man,
More white and red than doves or roses are;　　10
　　Nature that made thee with herself at strife
　　Saith that the world hath ending with thy life.

"Vouchsafe, thou wonder, to alight thy steed,
And rein his proud head to the saddle-bow;
If thou wilt deign this favor, for thy meed　　15
A thousand honey secrets shalt thou know.
　　Here come and sit, where never serpent hisses,
　　And being set, I'll smother thee with kisses;

19. **cloy:** surfeit; **satiety:** overindulgence.

24. **wasted:** expended.

26. **precedent:** sign; **pith and livelihood:** vigor and vitality. A moist palm was considered indicative of an amorous nature.

28. **sovereign:** supreme.

29. **enraged:** impassioned.

31. **courser's:** steed's.

32. **tender:** youthful.

34. **unapt to toy:** not in an amorous mood.

37. **ragged:** rough.

39. **stalled up:** secured; **even now:** at once.

40. **prove:** try.

43. **along:** prone (alongside him).

"And yet not cloy thy lips with loathed satiety,
But rather famish them amid their plenty,   20
Making them red and pale with fresh variety;
Ten kisses short as one, one long as twenty.
　A summer's day will seem an hour but short,
　Being wasted in such time-beguiling sport."

With this she seizeth on his sweating palm,   25
The precedent of pith and livelihood,
And, trembling in her passion, calls it balm,
Earth's sovereign salve to do a goddess good.
　Being so enraged, desire doth lend her force
　Courageously to pluck him from his horse.   30

Over one arm the lusty courser's rein,
Under her other was the tender boy,
Who blushed and pouted in a dull disdain,
With leaden appetite, unapt to toy;
　She red and hot as coals of glowing fire,   35
　He red for shame, but frosty in desire.

The studded bridle on a ragged bough
Nimbly she fastens—O, how quick is love!
The steed is stalled up, and even now
To tie the rider she begins to prove: 40
　Backward she pushed him, as she would be thrust,
　And governed him in strength, though not in lust.

So soon was she along as he was down,
Each leaning on their elbows and their hips;
Now doth she stroke his cheek, now doth he frown,   45

53. **miss:** misbehavior.
55. **sharp by fast:** ravenous from lack of food.
56. **Tires:** tears fiercely.
61. **Forced to content:** forced to be patient.
64. **air of grace:** divine breeze.
66. **So:** provided that; **distilling:** trickling.
67. **Look how:** just as.
71. **rank:** swollen.
72. **Perforce . . . force:** playing on the conventional phrase "force perforce."

An eagle with its prey. From Francis Barlow, *Various Birds and Beasts* (ca. 1755).

And 'gins to chide, but soon she stops his lips,
  And kissing speaks, with lustful language broken,
  "If thou wilt chide, thy lips shall never open."

He burns with bashful shame; she with her tears
Doth quench the maiden burning of his cheeks;   50
Then with her windy sighs and golden hairs
To fan and blow them dry again she seeks.
  He saith she is immodest, blames her miss;
  What follows more she murders with a kiss.

Even as an empty eagle, sharp by fast,   55
Tires with her beak on feathers, flesh and bone.
Shaking her wings, devouring all in haste,
Till either gorge be stuffed or prey be gone;
  Even so she kissed his brow, his cheek, his chin,
  And where she ends she doth anew begin.   60

Forced to content, but never to obey,
Panting he lies and breatheth in her face;
She feedeth on the steam as on a prey,
And calls it heavenly moisture, air of grace,
  Wishing her cheeks were gardens full of flowers,   65
  So they were dewed with such distilling showers.

Look how a bird lies tangled in a net,
So fastened in her arms Adonis lies;
Pure shame and awed resistance made him fret,
Which bred more beauty in his angry eyes.   70
  Rain added to a river that is rank
  Perforce will force it overflow the bank.

75. **lowers:** frowns.

82. **take truce:** make peace.

86. **dive-dapper:** dabchick; a small water bird.

90. **winks:** winces.

91. **passenger:** traveler.

94. **She bathes in water:** compare Sonnet 154: "Love's fire heats water; water cools not love."

98. **stern:** merciless.

Towns in Shakespeare's time, especially market towns, were frequently situated on rivers for ease of transportation. Floods were therefore a fairly common experience. Stratford-on-Avon suffered a severe flood in 1588, which may account for much of Shakespeare's flood imagery. From Daniel Cramer, *Octaginta emblemata* (1630).

Still she entreats, and prettily entreats,
For to a pretty ear she tunes her tale;
Still is he sullen, still he lowers and frets,　　　　75
'Twixt crimson shame and anger ashy-pale;
　　Being red, she loves him best, and being white,
　　Her best is bettered with a more delight.

Look how he can, she cannot choose but love;
And by her fair immortal hand she swears　　　　80
From his soft bosom never to remove
Till he take truce with her contending tears,
　　Which long have rained, making her cheeks all wet;
　　And one sweet kiss shall pay this countless debt.

Upon this promise did he raise his chin,　　　　85
Like a dive-dapper peering through a wave,
Who, being looked on, ducks as quickly in;
So offers he to give what she did crave;
　　But when her lips were ready for his pay,
　　He winks, and turns his lips another way.　　　　90

Never did passenger in summer's heat
More thirst for drink than she for this good turn.
Her help she sees, but help she cannot get;
She bathes in water, yet her fire must burn.
　　"O, pity," 'gan she cry, "flint-hearted boy!　　　　95
　　'Tis but a kiss I beg; why art thou coy?

"I have been wooed, as I entreat thee now,
Even by the stern and direful god of war,
Whose sinewy neck in battle ne'er did bow,

100. **jar:** conflict.

104. **uncontrolled crest:** helmet that has never bowed to a conqueror.

107. **churlish:** quarrelsome; **ensign:** standard.

114. **foiled:** defeated.

121. **wink:** close your eyes.

123. **twain:** two.

124. **in sight:** observed.

MARS;

"Over my altars hath he hung his lance,
His battered shield, his uncontrolled crest,
. . . .
Scorning his churlish drum and ensign red."
Mars, as pictured in Robert Whitcombe, *Janua divorum, or the Lives . . . of the Heathen Gods* (1678).

Who conquers where he comes in every jar; 100
   Yet hath he been my captive and my slave,
   And begged for that which thou unasked shalt have.

"Over my altars hath he hung his lance,
His battered shield, his uncontrolled crest,
And for my sake hath learned to sport and dance, 105
To toy, to wanton, dally, smile and jest,
   Scorning his churlish drum and ensign red,
   Making my arms his field, his tent my bed.

"Thus he that overruled I overswayed,
Leading him prisoner in a red-rose chain; 110
Strong-tempered steel his stronger strength obeyed,
Yet was he servile to my coy disdain.
   O, be not proud, nor brag not of thy might,
   For mast'ring her that foiled the god of fight!

"Touch but my lips with those fair lips of thine— 115
Though mine be not so fair, yet are they red—
The kiss shall be thine own as well as mine.
What see'st thou in the ground? Hold up thy head;
   Look in mine eyeballs, there thy beauty lies;
   Then why not lips on lips, since eyes in eyes? 120

"Art thou ashamed to kiss? Then wink again,
And I will wink; so shall the day seem night.
Love keeps his revels where there are but twain;
Be bold to play, our sport is not in sight.
   These blue-veined violets whereon we lean 125
   Never can blab, nor know not what we mean.

127. **tender spring:** young beard.

133. **hard-favored:** ugly; **foul:** disagreeable.

134. **Ill-nurtured:** rude.

135. **O'erworn:** debilitated by age.

136. **juice:** youthful sap.

140. **grey:** luminous.

141. **as:** like.

145. **discourse:** talk.

148. **no footing seen:** i.e., so lightly as to leave no print.

149. **all compact of:** fully composed of.

150. **gross:** heavy; **aspire:** rise skyward.

151. **Witness:** accept as witness.

A sea nymph "with long dishevelled hair."
From Geoffrey Whitney, *A Choice of Emblems* (1586).

"The tender spring upon thy tempting lip
Shows thee unripe; yet mayst thou well be tasted;
Make use of time, let not advantage slip;
Beauty within itself should not be wasted.　　　　130
　　Fair flowers that are not gathered in their prime
　　Rot and consume themselves in little time.

"Were I hard-favored, foul, or wrinkled-old,
Ill-nurtured, crooked, churlish, harsh in voice,
O'erworn, despised, rheumatic and cold,　　　　135
Thick-sighted, barren, lean, and lacking juice,
　　Then mightst thou pause, for then I were not for
　　　　thee;
　　But having no defects, why dost abhor me?

"Thou canst not see one wrinkle in my brow;
Mine eyes are grey and bright and quick in turning; 140
My beauty as the spring doth yearly grow,
My flesh is soft and plump, my marrow burning;
　　My smooth moist hand, were it with thy hand felt,
　　Would in thy palm dissolve, or seem to melt.

"Bid me discourse, I will enchant thine ear,　　　　145
Or, like a fairy, trip upon the green,
Or, like a nymph, with long dishevelled hair,
Dance on the sands, and yet no footing seen.
　　Love is a spirit all compact of fire,
　　Not gross to sink, but light, and will aspire.　　　　150

"Witness this primrose bank whereon I lie;
These forceless flowers like sturdy trees support me;
Two strengthless doves will draw me through the sky

154. **list:** desire.

156. **heavy:** burdensome; tedious.

157. **affected:** inclined lovingly.

160. **on:** of.

161. **Narcissus:** In Greek mythology, Narcissus was a beautiful youth who fell in love with his own reflection in a pool and died pining for himself.

165. **sappy:** fruitful. This and the next stanza repeat the theme of Sonnets 1-17.

166. **to themselves:** alone; without self-reproduction.

169. **increase:** offspring; fruits.

177. **Titan:** i.e., Helios, the sun-god.

"Narcissus so himself himself forsook,
And died to kiss his shadow in the brook"
From Whitney's *A Choice of Emblems* (1586).

From morn till night, even where I list to sport me.
  Is love so light, sweet boy, and may it be   155
  That thou should think it heavy unto thee?

"Is thine own heart to thine own face affected?
Can thy right hand seize love upon thy left?
Then woo thyself, be of thyself rejected,
Steal thine own freedom, and complain on theft.   160
  Narcissus so himself himself forsook,
  And died to kiss his shadow in the brook.

"Torches are made to light, jewels to wear,
Dainties to taste, fresh beauty for the use,
Herbs for their smell, and sappy plants to bear;   165
Things growing to themselves are growth's abuse.
  Seeds spring from seeds and beauty breedeth
     beauty;
  Thou wast begot; to get it is thy duty.

"Upon the earth's increase why shouldst thou feed,
Unless the earth with thy increase be fed?   170
By law of nature thou art bound to breed,
That thine may live when thou thyself art dead;
  And so in spite of death thou dost survive,
  In that thy likeness still is left alive."

By this, the love-sick queen began to sweat,   175
For where they lay the shadow had forsook them,
And Titan, tired in the mid-day heat,
With burning eye did hotly overlook them,
  Wishing Adonis had his team to guide,
  So he were like him, and by Venus' side.   180

181. **sprite:** spirit.

182. **heavy:** melancholy.

185. **Souring:** spoiling.

200. **stone at rain relenteth:** proverbial: "Constant dropping will wear the stone."

204. **unkind:** although a conventional adjective for an unyielding mistress, there may be present some such sense as "childless," lacking "kind" in the sense of "offspring."

205. **contemn:** scorn; **this:** thus.

The sun-god Titan, also known as Helios in early Greek mythology, was thought to drive his chariot and team of four horses across the sky each day from dawn to sunset. From Claude Menestrier, *L'art des emblemes* (1648).

And now Adonis, with a lazy sprite,
And with a heavy, dark, disliking eye,
His lowering brows o'erwhelming his fair sight,
Like misty vapors when they blot the sky,
    Souring his cheeks, cries "Fie, no more of love!   185
    The sun doth burn my face; I must remove."

"Ay me," quoth Venus, "young, and so unkind!
What bare excuses mak'st thou to be gone!
I'll sigh celestial breath, whose gentle wind
Shall cool the heat of this descending sun;   190
    I'll make a shadow for thee of my hairs;
    If they burn too, I'll quench them with my tears.

"The sun that shines from heaven shines but warm,
And lo, I lie between that sun and thee;
The heat I have from thence doth little harm;   195
Thine eye darts forth the fire that burneth me;
    And were I not immortal, life were done
    Between this heavenly and earthly sun.

"Art thou obdurate, flinty, hard as steel?
Nay, more than flint, for stone at rain relenteth.   200
Art thou a woman's son, and canst not feel
What 'tis to love, how want of love tormenteth?
    O, had thy mother borne so hard a mind,
    She had not brought forth thee, but died unkind.

"What am I that thou shouldst contemn me this?   205
Or what great danger dwells upon my suit?
What were thy lips the worse for one poor kiss?

215. **complexion:** appearance.

218. **passion:** anger.

219. **blaze:** (1) flame; (2) blazon (heraldic).

220. **Being judge in love:** although love cases come under her jurisdiction.

221. **fain:** willingly.

222. **intendments:** purposes.

229. **Fondling:** fool.

230. **pale:** fence (her arms).

"No dog shall rouse thee, though a thousand bark."
From Barlow, *Various Birds* (ca. 1755).

Speak, fair; but speak fair words, or else be mute.
  Give me one kiss, I'll give it thee again,
  And one for int'rest, if thou wilt have twain.   210

"Fie, lifeless picture, cold and senseless stone,
Well painted idol, image dull and dead,
Statue contenting but the eye alone,
Thing like a man, but of no woman bred!
  Thou art no man, though of a man's complexion, 215
  For men will kiss even by their own direction."

This said, impatience chokes her pleading tongue,
And swelling passion doth provoke a pause;
Red cheeks and fiery eyes blaze forth her wrong;
Being judge in love, she cannot right her cause;   220
  And now she weeps, and now she fain would speak,
  And now her sobs do her intendments break.

Sometime she shakes her head, and then his hand,
Now gazeth she on him, now on the ground;
Sometime her arms infold him like a band;   225
She would, he will not in her arms be bound;
  And when from thence he struggles to be gone,
  She locks her lily fingers one in one.

"Fondling," she saith, "since I have hemmed thee here
Within the circuit of this ivory pale,   230
I'll be a park, and thou shalt be my deer;
Feed where thou wilt, on mountain or in dale;
  Graze on my lips, and if those hills be dry,
  Stray lower, where the pleasant fountains lie.

235. **relief:** food.

236. **bottom:** valley.

237. **brakes:** thickets.

240. **rouse:** rout out.

241. **as:** as if.

242. **That:** so that.

243. **if:** so that if.

246. **there Love lived:** i.e., the dimples were so bewitching as to inspire love in the beholder.

251. **in thine own law forlorn:** made wretched by something for which she herself has made the rules.

257. **remorse:** compassion.

259. **copse:** thicket.

260. **jennet:** small Spanish horse; **proud:** erotically excited.

"A breeding jennet, lusty, young and proud"
From George Vertue, *A Description of the Works of . . . Wenceslaus Hollar* (1759).

"Within this limit is relief enough,   235
Sweet bottom-grass and high delightful plain,
Round rising hillocks, brakes obscure and rough,
To shelter thee from tempest and from rain:
    Then be my deer, since I am such a park;
    No dog shall rouse thee, though a thousand bark." 240

At this Adonis smiles as in disdain,
That in each cheek appears a pretty dimple.
Love made those hollows, if himself were slain,
He might be buried in a tomb so simple;
    Foreknowing well, if there he came to lie,   245
    Why, there Love lived, and there he could not die.

These lovely caves, these round enchanting pits,
Opened their mouths to swallow Venus' liking.
Being mad before, how doth she now for wits?
Struck dead at first, what needs a second striking?   250
    Poor queen of love, in thine own law forlorn,
    To love a cheek that smiles at thee in scorn!

Now which way shall she turn? What shall she say?
Her words are done, her woes the more increasing;
The time is spent, her object will away,   255
And from her twining arms doth urge releasing.
    "Pity," she cries, "some favor, some remorse!"
    Away he springs, and hasteth to his horse.

But lo, from forth a copse that neighbors by,
A breeding jennet, lusty, young and proud,   260
Adonis' trampling courser doth espy,

266. **woven girths:** straps to fasten saddle or blanket on a horse's back.

267. **bearing:** a play on "enduring" (submissive) and "productive"?

272. **compassed:** arched.

275. **glisters:** gleams.

276. **courage:** lust.

277. **told:** counted.

279. **curvets:** prances.

280. **tried:** proved.

283. **recketh he:** does he care for.

284. **flattering "Holla":** wheedling request to "whoa."

285. **curb:** bit.

286. **caparisons:** synonymous with *trappings*.

288. **with . . . agrees:** is agreeable to.

"Adonis' trampling courser doth espy"
From Arnold Freitag, *Mythologia ethica* (1579).

13

And forth she rushes, snorts and neighs aloud.
  The strong-necked steed, being tied unto a tree,
  Breaketh his rein and to her straight goes he.

Imperiously he leaps, he neighs, he bounds,   265
And now his woven girths he breaks asunder;
The bearing earth with his hard hoof he wounds,
Whose hollow womb resounds like heaven's thunder;
  The iron bit he crusheth 'tween his teeth,
  Controlling what he was controlled with.   270

His ears up-pricked; his braided hanging mane
Upon his compassed crest now stand on end;
His nostrils drink the air, and forth again,
As from a furnace, vapors doth he send;
  His eye, which scornfully glisters like fire,   275
  Shows his hot courage and his high desire.

Sometime he trots, as if he told the steps,
With gentle majesty and modest pride;
Anon he rears upright, curvets and leaps,
As who should say "Lo, thus my strength is tried,   280
  And this I do to captivate the eye
  Of the fair breeder that is standing by."

What recketh he his rider's angry stir,
His flattering "Holla" or his "Stand, I say"?
What cares he now for curb or pricking spur?   285
For rich caparisons or trappings gay?
  He sees his love, and nothing else he sees,
  For nothing else with his proud sight agrees.

289. **Look when:** whenever.
290. **limning:** painting.
295. **fetlocks:** tufts of hair above the horse's heel.
297. **passing:** surpassingly.
301. **scuds:** run swiftly.
303. **bid the wind a base:** challenge the wind to a chase, as in the game "prisoner's base."
304. **where:** whether; **whether:** which.
310. **strangeness:** coldness.
313. **malcontent:** disgruntled fellow.
314. **vails:** droops.

Look when a painter would surpass the life
In limning out a well-proportioned steed,   290
His art with nature's workmanship at strife,
As if the dead the living should exceed;
    So did this horse excel a common one
    In shape, in courage, color, pace and bone.

Round-hoofed, short-jointed, fetlocks shag and long,   295
Broad breast, full eye, small head and nostril wide,
High crest, short ears, straight legs and passing strong,
Thin mane, thick tail, broad buttock, tender hide;
    Look what a horse should have he did not lack,
    Save a proud rider on so proud a back.   300

Sometime he scuds far off, and there he stares;
Anon he starts at stirring of a feather;
To bid the wind a base he now prepares,
And where he run or fly they know not whether;
    For through his mane and tail the high wind sings,   305
    Fanning the hairs, who wave like feathered wings.

He looks upon his love and neighs unto her;
She answers him as if she knew his mind;
Being proud, as females are, to see him woo her,
She puts on outward strangeness, seems unkind,   310
    Spurns at his love and scorns the heat he feels,
    Beating his kind embracements with her heels.

Then, like a melancholy malcontent,
He vails his tail, that, like a falling plume,
Cool shadow to his melting buttock lent;   315

319. **goeth about:** tries.

321. **Jealous of catching:** fearful of being caught.

325. **chafing:** anger.

326. **Banning:** cursing; **boist'rous:** rebellious.

335. **heart's attorney:** i.e., the tongue.

336. **The client breaks:** compare *Macbeth*, IV. iii.: "The grief that does not speak/ Whispers the o'erfraught heart and bids it break."

339. **bonnet:** hat.

342. **all askance:** i.e., out of the corner of his eye.

He stamps, and bites the poor flies in his fume.
  His love, perceiving how he was enraged,
  Grew kinder, and his fury was assuaged.

His testy master goeth about to take him,
When, lo, the unbacked breeder, full of fear,   320
Jealous of catching, swiftly doth forsake him,
With her the horse, and left Adonis there.
  As they were mad, unto the wood they hie them,
  Out-stripping crows that strive to over-fly them.

All swol'n with chafing, down Adonis sits,   325
Banning his boist'rous and unruly beast;
And now the happy season once more fits
That love-sick Love by pleading may be blest;
  For lovers say the heart hath treble wrong
  When it is barred the aidance of the tongue.   330

An oven that is stopped, or river stayed,
Burneth more hotly, swelleth with more rage;
So of concealed sorrow may be said,
Free vent of words love's fire doth assuage;
  But when the heart's attorney once is mute,   335
  The client breaks, as desperate in his suit.

He sees her coming, and begins to glow,
Even as a dying coal revives with wind,
And with his bonnet hides his angry brow,
Looks on the dull earth with disturbed mind,   340
  Taking no notice that she is so nigh,
  For all askance he holds her in his eye.

343. **wistly:** intently.
354. **apt:** readily; **dint:** impression.
359. **his:** its.
362. **gaol:** jail.
363. **alablaster:** alabaster.
364. **engirts:** encloses.
365. **willful:** lustful.
366. **Showed:** resembled.
367. **engine:** instrument; her tongue.
368. **mortal round:** earth.

O, what a sight it was, wistly to view
How she came stealing to the wayward boy!
To note the fighting conflict of her hue,   345
How white and red each other did destroy!
    But now her cheek was pale, and by and by
    It flashed forth fire, as lightning from the sky.

Now was she just before him as he sat,
And like a lowly lover down she kneels;   350
With one fair hand she heaveth up his hat,
Her other tender hand his fair cheek feels;
    His tend'rer cheek receives her soft hand's **print**
    As apt as new-fall'n snow takes any dint.

O, what a war of looks was then between them,   355
Her eyes petitioners to his eyes suing!
His eyes saw her eyes as they had not seen them;
Her eyes wooed still, his eyes disdained the wooing;
    And all this dumb play had his acts made plain
    With tears which chorus-like her eyes did rain.   360

Full gently now she takes him by the hand,
A lily prisoned in a gaol of snow,
Or ivory in an alablaster band;
So white a friend engirts so white a foe:
    This beauteous combat, willful and unwilling,   365
    Showed like two silver doves that sit a-billing.

Once more the engine of her thoughts began:
"O fairest mover on this mortal round,
Would thou wert as I am, and I a man,

370. **my wound:** wounded like mine.
372. **bane:** destruction.
376. **grave it:** make a mark on it.
384. **palfrey:** horse.
388. **suffered:** permitted; allowed to continue.
390. **though:** if.
391. **jade:** tired nag.
393. **fee:** right; due.
396. **Enfranchising:** setting free.

My heart all whole as thine, thy heart my wound;   370
  For one sweet look thy help I would assure thee,
  Though nothing but my body's bane would cure
      thee."

"Give me my hand," saith he; "why dost thou feel it?"
"Give me my heart," saith she, "and thou shalt have it;
O, give it me, lest thy hard heart do steel it,   375
And being steeled, soft sighs can never grave it;
  Then love's deep groans I never shall regard,
  Because Adonis' heart hath made mine hard."

"For shame," he cries, "let go, and let me go;
My day's delight is past, my horse is gone,   380
And 'tis your fault I am bereft him so.
I pray you hence, and leave me here alone;
  For all my mind, my thought, my busy care,
  Is how to get my palfrey from the mare."

Thus she replies: "Thy palfrey, as he should,   385
Welcomes the warm approach of sweet desire.
Affection is a coal that must be cooled;
Else, suffered, it will set the heart on fire.
  The sea hath bounds, but deep desire hath none,
  Therefore no marvel though thy horse be gone.   390

"How like a jade he stood tied to the tree,
Servilely mastered with a leathern rein!
But when he saw his love, his youth's fair fee,
He held such petty bondage in disdain,
  Throwing the base thong from his bending crest,   395
  Enfranchising his mouth, his back, his breast.

400. **agents:** senses.

405. **on:** of; **presented:** proffered.

407. **but plain:** not difficult.

408. **made perfect:** perfectly learned.

410. **boar:** fierce, wild, male hog.

412. **My love to love is love but to disgrace it:** the only affection love inspires in me is a liking to ridicule it.

417. **springing:** new-sprung; youthful.

418. **prime:** springtime; first youth; **nothing worth:** worthless.

420. **pride:** strength.

422. **idle:** worthless; **bootless:** unprofitable.

"Who sees his true-love in her naked bed,
Teaching the sheets a whiter hue than white,
But, when his glutton eye so full hath fed,
His other agents aim at like delight?   400
    Who is so faint that dares not be so bold
    To touch the fire, the weather being cold?

"Let me excuse thy courser, gentle boy;
And learn of him, I heartily beseech thee,
To take advantage on presented joy;   405
Though I were dumb, yet his proceedings teach thee.
    O, learn to love; the lesson is but plain,
    And once made perfect, never lost again."

"I know not love," quoth he, "nor will not know it,
Unless it be a boar, and then I chase it.   410
'Tis much to borrow, and I will not owe it.
My love to love is love but to disgrace it;
    For I have heard it is a life in death,
    That laughs, and weeps, and all but with a breath.

"Who wears a garment shapeless and unfinished?   415
Who plucks the bud before one leaf put forth?
If springing things be any jot diminished,
They wither in their prime, prove nothing worth.
    The colt that's backed and burdened being young
    Loseth his pride, and never waxeth strong.   420

"You hurt my hand with wringing; let us part,
And leave this idle theme, this bootless chat;
Remove your siege from my unyielding heart;

426. **batt'ry:** violent entrance.

429. **mermaid's:** siren's.

430. **now pressed with bearing:** and am now crushed under the weight I have to bear; i.e., the earlier load was Adonis' unresponsiveness, to which is now added a downright verbal rejection.

433-47. Sonnet 141 is almost an inversion of the sense of these lines.

434. **inward beauty and invisible:** i.e., beauty of voice, which cannot be seen but is perceived within the ear.

436. **sensible:** receptive to impressions of the senses.

443. **stillitory:** still; **face excelling:** surpassingly beautiful face.

To love's alarms it will not ope the gate.
　Dismiss your vows, your feigned tears, your 425
　　flatt'ry;
　For where a heart is hard they make no batt'ry."

"What, canst thou talk?" quoth she. "Hast thou a
　　tongue?
O, would thou hadst not, or I had no hearing!
Thy mermaid's voice hath done me double wrong;
I had my load before, now pressed with bearing:　430
　Melodious discord, heavenly tune harsh sounding,
　Ears' deep-sweet music, and heart's deep-sore
　　wounding.

"Had I no eyes but ears, my ears would love
That inward beauty and invisible;
Or were I deaf, thy outward parts would move　435
Each part in me that were but sensible.
　Though neither eyes nor ears, to hear nor see,
　Yet should I be in love by touching thee.

"Say that the sense of feeling were bereft me,
And that I could not see, nor hear, nor touch,　440
And nothing but the very smell were left me,
Yet would my love to thee be still as much;
　For from the stillitory of thy face excelling
　Comes breath perfumed, that breedeth love by
　　smelling.

"But O, what banquet wert thou to the taste,　445
Being nurse and feeder of the other four!
Would they not wish the feast might ever last,

453. Like a red morn: An echo of a proverb still in current use in several versions: "Red in the west, sailor's rest;/ Red in the morning, sailor take warning."

454. Wrack: disaster.

456. flaws: blasts of wind.

457. presage: foretelling; **advisedly:** thoughtfully.

459. grin: bare his teeth.

464. by looks reviveth: i.e., is rekindled by looking at the beloved.

465. recures: cures.

466. bankrout: bankrupt.

467. silly: innocent.

469. brake: broke.

471. wittily: cleverly.

472. Fair fall: fair befall; good luck to.

473. as: as if.

Jealousy, "that sour unwelcome guest"
From Whitney's *A Choice of Emblems* (1586).

And bid Suspicion double-lock the door,
　Lest Jealousy, that sour unwelcome guest,
　Should by his stealing in disturb the feast?"　　　450

Once more the ruby-colored portal opened,
Which to his speech did honey passage yield;
Like a red morn, that ever yet betokened
Wrack to the seaman, tempest to the field,
　Sorrow to shepherds, woe unto the birds,　　　455
　Gusts and foul flaws to herdmen and to herds.

This ill presage advisedly she marketh.
Even as the wind is hushed before it raineth,
Or as the wolf doth grin before he barketh,
Or as the berry breaks before it staineth,　　　460
　Or like the deadly bullet of a gun,
　His meaning struck her ere his words begun.

And at his look she flatly falleth down,
For looks kill love, and love by looks reviveth;
A smile recures the wounding of a frown.　　　465
But blessed bankrout that by love so thriveth!
　The silly boy, believing she is dead,
　Claps her pale cheek, till clapping makes its red;

And all amazed brake off his late intent,
For sharply he did think to reprehend her,　　　470
Which cunning love did wittily prevent.
Fair fall the wit that can so well defend her!
　For on the grass she lies as she were slain,
　Till his breath breatheth life in her again.

480. **still:** ever.

482. **windows:** eyes.

490. **repine:** unhappiness.

497. **life was death's annoy:** life was as painful as death.

498. **lively:** lifegiving.

500. **shrewd:** severe; malicious.

APOLLO

". . . as the bright sun glorifies the sky"
In later classical mythology Apollo, god of radiance and light, came to be identified with Titan, properly the sun-god. From Whitcombe, *Janua divorum* (1678).

He wrings her nose, he strikes her on the cheeks, 475
He bends her fingers, holds her pulses hard,
He chafes her lips, a thousand ways he seeks
To mend the hurt that his unkindness marred;
  He kisses her; and she, by her good will,
  Will never rise, so he will kiss her still. 480

The night of sorrow now is turned to day:
Her two blue windows faintly she upheaveth,
Like the fair sun, when in his fresh array
He cheers the morn, and all the earth relieveth;
  And as the bright sun glorifies the sky, 485
  So is her face illumined with her eye;

Whose beams upon his hairless face are fixed,
As if from thence they borrowed all their shine.
Were never four such lamps together mixed,
Had not his clouded with his brow's repine; 490
  But hers, which through the crystal tears gave light,
  Shone like the moon in water seen by night.

"O, where am I?" quoth she, "in earth or heaven,
Or in the ocean drenched, or in the fire?
What hour is this? or morn or weary even? 495
Do I delight to die, or life desire?
  But now I lived, and life was death's annoy;
  But now I died, and death was lively joy.

"O, thou didst kill me: kill me once again.
Thy eyes' shrewd tutor, that hard heart of thine, 500
Hath taught them scornful tricks, and such disdain

505. **for:** i.e., as a reward for.

506. **wear:** wear out; deteriorate.

507. **verdure:** freshness.

510. **breath:** the sweetness of his breath may serve like the sweet-smelling herbs that were believed to ward off infection from the plague.

515. **slips:** counterfeits.

519. **touches:** impressions from the lips; kisses.

520. **told:** counted.

523. **owe:** bear.

524. **strangeness:** coldness.

526. **ungrown fry:** young fish.

A stargazer, or astrologer. From Jean Jacques Boissard, *Icones quinquaginta virorum* (1597-99).

That they have murdered this poor heart of mine;
  And these mine eyes, true leaders to their queen,
  But for thy piteous lips no more had seen.

"Long may they kiss each other, for this cure!   505
O, never let their crimson liveries wear!
And as they last, their verdure still endure
To drive infection from the dangerous year!
  That the star-gazers, having writ on death,
  May say, the plague is banished by thy breath.   510

"Pure lips, sweet seals in my soft lips imprinted,
What bargains may I make, still to be sealing?
To sell myself I can be well contented,
So thou wilt buy, and pay, and use good dealing;
  Which purchase if thou make, for fear of slips   515
  Set thy seal manual on my wax-red lips.

"A thousand kisses buys my heart from me;
And pay them at thy leisure, one by one.
What is ten hundred touches unto thee?
Are they not quickly told and quickly gone?   520
  Say for non-payment that the debt should double,
  Is twenty hundred kisses such a trouble?"

"Fair queen," quoth he, "if any love you owe me,
Measure my strangeness with my unripe years;
Before I know myself, seek not to know me;   525
No fisher but the ungrown fry forbears.
  The mellow plum doth fall, the green sticks fast,
  Or being early plucked is sour to taste.

529. **world's comforter:** the sun.
538. **tendered:** offered.
540. **Incorporate:** grown into one body.
544. **on:** of.
545. **pressed:** oppressed.
550. **insulter:** exultant victor.
551. **vulture:** ravenous.

"The owl, night's herald, shrieks . . ."
From Ulisse Aldrovandi, *Ornithologiae* (1599-1603).

"Look, the world's comforter, with weary gait,
His day's hot task hath ended in the west;   530
The owl, night's herald, shrieks 'tis very late;
The sheep are gone to fold, birds to their nest;
  And coal-black clouds that shadow heaven's light
  Do summon us to part, and bid good night.

"Now let me say 'Good night', and so say you;   535
If you will say so, you shall have a kiss."
"Good night," quoth she; and, ere he says "Adieu,"
The honey fee of parting tendered is:
  Her arms do lend his neck a sweet embrace;
  Incorporate then they seem; face grows to face.   540

Till breathless he disjoined, and backward drew
The heavenly moisture, that sweet coral mouth,
Whose precious taste her thirsty lips well knew,
Whereon they surfeit, yet complain on drouth.
  He with her plenty pressed, she faint with dearth,   545
  Their lips together glued, fall to the earth.

Now quick desire hath caught the yielding prey,
And glutton-like she feeds, yet never filleth;
Her lips are conquerors, his lips obey,
Paying what ransom the insulter willeth;   550
  Whose vulture thought doth pitch the price so high
  That she will draw his lips' rich treasure dry.

And having felt the sweetness of the spoil,
With blindfold fury she begins to forage;
Her face doth reek and smoke, her blood doth boil,   555

556. **careless:** rash.

561. **roe:** deer.

562. **froward:** naughty.

564. **listeth:** wishes.

565. **temp'ring:** handling.

567. **compassed:** achieved.

568. **Chiefly:** especially; **whose leave exceeds commission:** i.e., which will not submit to restraints.

569. **Affection:** desire.

570. **froward:** adverse; unwilling.

573. **Foul:** unpleasant.

AMORVM. 195

Bb 2

Cupid with his bow, stepping upon pride. From Octavio van Veen, *Amorum emblemata* (1608).

And careless lust stirs up a desperate courage,
  Planting oblivion, beating reason back,
  Forgetting shame's pure blush and honor's wrack.

Hot, faint and weary, with her hard embracing,
Like a wild bird being tamed with too much handling, 560
Or as the fleet-foot roe that's tired with chasing,
Or like the froward infant stilled with dandling,
  He now obeys and now no more resisteth,
  While she takes all she can, not all she listeth.

What wax so frozen but dissolves with temp'ring, 565
And yields at last to every light impression?
Things out of hope are compassed oft with vent'ring,
Chiefly in love, whose leave exceeds commission:
  Affection faints not like a pale-faced coward,
  But then woos best when most his choice is froward. 570

When he did frown, O, had she then gave over,
Such nectar from his lips she had not sucked.
Foul words and frowns must not repel a lover;
What though the rose have prickles, yet 'tis plucked.
  Were beauty under twenty locks kept fast, 575
  Yet love breaks through, and picks them all at last.

For pity now she can no more detain him;
The poor fool prays her that he may depart.
She is resolved no longer to restrain him;
Bids him farewell, and look well to her heart, 580
  The which by Cupid's bow she doth protest
  He carries thence incaged in his breast.

583. **waste:** spend.

584. **watch:** remain wakeful.

586. **match:** bargain.

590. **Like lawn . . . rose:** the sense is that her cheeks turned pale as if covered with sheer white cambric; i.e., *lawn*.

597. **All is imaginary she doth prove:** i.e., the conflict is all in her imagination.

598. **manage:** a technical term meaning to put a horse through its paces.

599. **Tantalus:** Zeus punished Tantalus in the afterlife by having him placed in a lake, whose waters receded when he tried to drink, while overhead hung branches of fruit, which he was unable to reach. Cf. "tantalize," which derives from Tantalus' punishment; **annoy:** agony.

600. **clip Elysium:** embrace paradise.

601. **poor birds, deceived with painted grapes:** referring to a tale in Pliny concerning the painter Zeuxis, which was repeated by several contemporary works with which Shakespeare was familiar.

602. **pine the maw:** starve the stomach.

604. **helpless:** unhelpful.

608. **proved:** tried.

"Sweet boy," she says, "this night I'll waste in sorrow,
For my sick heart commands mine eyes to watch.
Tell me, love's master, shall we meet tomorrow?   585
Say, shall we? Shall we? Wilt thou make the match?"
     He tells her, no; tomorrow he intends
     To hunt the boar with certain of his friends.

"The boar!" quoth she; whereat a sudden pale,
Like lawn being spread upon the blushing rose,   590
Usurps her cheek; she trembles at his tale,
And on his neck her yoking arms she throws.
     She sinketh down, still hanging by his neck,
     He on her belly falls, she on her back.

Now is she in the very lists of love,   595
Her champion mounted for the hot encounter.
All is imaginary she doth prove;
He will not manage her, although he mount her;
     That worse than Tantalus' is her annoy,
     To clip Elysium and to lack her joy.   600

Even so poor birds, deceived with painted grapes,
Do surfeit by the eye and pine the maw;
Even so she languisheth in her mishaps
As those poor birds that helpless berries saw.
     The warm effects which she in him finds missing   605
     She seeks to kindle with continual kissing.

But all in vain, good queen, it will not be.
She hath assayed as much as may be proved;
Her pleading hath deserved a greater fee;

615. **be advised:** take care.

617. **tushes:** variant of tusks, still in colloquial use in certain parts of the United States.

618. **mortal:** deadly; **bent to kill:** intent upon killing.

619. **bow back:** arched back; **battle:** battle array.

623. **moved:** angered.

625. **brawny:** lean and muscular.

626. **better proof:** more impenetrable.

628. **venter:** venture.

633. **eyne:** eyes.

635. **at vantage:** conveniently placed for attack.

636. **root:** gore with his tusks; **mead:** meadow.

"With javelin's point a churlish swine to gore"
Boar hunting. From Lodovico Dolce, *Le trasformationi* (1558).

She's Love, she loves, and yet she is not loved.   610
  "Fie, fie," he says, "you crush me; let me go;
  You have no reason to withhold me so."

"Thou hadst been gone," quoth she, "sweet boy, ere
   this,
But that thou told'st me thou wouldst hunt the boar.
O, be advised: thou know'st not what it is   615
With javelin's point a churlish swine to gore,
  Whose tushes never sheathed he whetteth still,
  Like to a mortal butcher bent to kill.

"On his bow back he hath a battle set
Of bristly pikes that ever threat his foes;   620
His eyes like glowworms shine when he doth fret;
His snout digs sepulchers where'er he goes;
  Being moved, he strikes whate'er is in his way,
  And whom he strikes his crooked tushes slay.

"His brawny sides, with hairy bristles armed,   625
Are better proof than thy spear's point can enter;
His short thick neck cannot be easily harmed;
Being ireful, on the lion he will venter:
  The thorny brambles and embracing bushes,
  As fearful of him, part; through whom he rushes.   630

"Alas, he nought esteems that face of thine,
To which Love's eyes pays tributary gazes;
Nor thy soft hands, sweet lips and crystal eyne,
Whose full perfection all the world amazes;
  But having thee at vantage—wondrous dread!—   635
  Would root these beauties as he roots the mead.

637. **cabin:** den.

641. **not to dissemble:** truthfully.

645. **downright:** at once.

647. **boding:** foretelling.

649. **Jealousy:** watchful care.

651. **suggesteth:** incites.

653. **Distemp'ring:** unsettling.

655. **sour:** disagreeable; **bate-breeding:** trouble-making.

656. **canker:** cankerworm; **spring:** sprout.

657. **carry-tale:** tattletale; **dissentious:** quarrelsome.

Jealousy, who
"Gives false alarms, suggesteth mutiny,
    And in a peaceful hour doth cry 'Kill, kill!'"
From Vincenzo Cartari's *Imagini de gli dei delli antichi* (1615).

"O, let him keep his loathsome cabin still;
Beauty hath nought to do with such foul fiends.
Come not within his danger by thy will;
They that thrive well take counsel of their friends.   640
    When thou didst name the boar, not to dissemble,
    I feared thy fortune, and my joints did tremble.

"Didst thou not mark my face? Was it not white?
Saw'st thou not signs of fear lurk in mine eye?
Grew I not faint? and fell I not downright?   645
Within my bosom, whereon thou dost lie,
    My boding heart pants, beats, and takes no rest,
    But, like an earthquake, shakes thee on my breast.

"For where Love reigns, disturbing Jealousy
Doth call himself Affection's sentinel;   650
Gives false alarms, suggesteth mutiny,
And in a peaceful hour doth cry 'Kill, kill!'
    Distemp'ring gentle Love in his desire,
    As air and water do abate the fire.

"This sour informer, this bate-breeding spy,   655
This canker that eats up Love's tender spring,
This carry-tale, dissentious Jealousy,
That sometime true news, sometime false doth bring,
    Knocks at my heart, and whispers in mine ear
    That if I love thee I thy death should fear;   660

"And more than so, presenteth to mine eye
The picture of an angry chafing boar
Under whose sharp fangs on his back doth lie

672. **encounter:** contend.

674. **Uncouple:** loose your dogs.

678. **well-breathed:** not short of wind.

679. **purblind:** dimsighted.

680. **overshoot:** outrun.

682. **cranks:** winds; **crosses:** crisscrosses his own tracks.

683. **musits:** openings in fences and hedges.

684. **amaze:** bewilder.

687. **earth-delving:** burrowing; **conies:** rabbits.

688. **their yell:** baying of hounds.

689. **sorteth:** consorteth; associates.

690. **shifts:** tricks; **wit waits on:** ingenuity serves.

An image like thyself, all stained with gore;
  Whose blood upon the fresh flowers being shed   665
  Doth make them droop with grief and hang the
    head.

"What should I do, seeing thee so indeed,
That tremble at th'imagination?
The thought of it doth make my faint heart bleed,
And fear doth teach it divination: 670
  I prophesy thy death, my living sorrow,
  If thou encounter with the boar tomorrow.

"But if thou needs wilt hunt, be ruled by me;
Uncouple at the timorous flying hare,
Or at the fox which lives by subtlety,   675
Or at the roe which no encounter dare.
  Pursue these fearful creatures o'er the downs,
  And on thy well-breathed horse keep with thy
    hounds.

"And when thou hast on foot the purblind hare,
Mark the poor wretch, to overshoot his troubles,   680
How he outruns the wind, and with what care
He cranks and crosses with a thousand doubles.
  The many musits through the which he goes
  Are like a labyrinth to amaze his foes.

"Sometime he runs among a flock of sheep,   685
To make the cunning hounds mistake their smell,
And sometime where earth-delving conies keep,
To stop the loud pursuers in their yell;
  And sometime sorteth with a herd of deer.
  Danger deviseth shifts; wit waits on fear.   690

694. **fault:** scent; **cleanly:** precisely.
695. **spend their mouths:** begin to bay again.
697. **Wat:** a traditional name for a hare.
700. **alarums:** alarms.
702. **sore:** grievously; **passing-bell:** death knell.
704. **indenting:** zigzagging.
705. **envious:** malicious.
714. **comment:** expatiate.
715. **leave:** leave off; i.e., what was I saying?
716. **aptly:** suitably.

"For there his smell with others being mingled,
The hot scent-snuffing hounds are driven to doubt,
Ceasing their clamorous cry till they have singled
With much ado the cold fault cleanly out.
　　Then do they spend their mouths; Echo replies,　695
　　As if another chase were in the skies.

"By this, poor Wat, far off upon a hill,
Stands on his hinder legs with list'ning ear,
To hearken if his foes pursue him still;
Anon their loud alarums he doth hear;　　　　700
　　And now his grief may be compared well
　　To one sore sick that hears the passing-bell.

"Then shalt thou see the dew-bedabbled wretch
Turn, and return, indenting with the way;
Each envious brier his weary legs do scratch,　705
Each shadow makes him stop, each murmur stay;
　　For misery is trodden on by many,
　　And being low never relieved by any.

"Lie quietly and hear a little more;
Nay, do not struggle, for thou shalt not rise.　710
To make thee hate the hunting of the boar,
Unlike myself thou hear'st me moralize,
　　Applying this to that, and so to so;
　　For love can comment upon every woe.

"Where did I leave?" "No matter where," quoth he;　715
"Leave me, and then the story aptly ends.
The night is spent." "Why, what of that?" quoth she.

724. **true:** honest.

725. **Dian:** the chaste goddess Diana; **cloudy:** melancholy; **forlorn:** lonely.

726. **forsworn:** an oathbreaker, being sworn to virginity.

728. **Cynthia:** another name for Diana as moon-goddess.

729. **forging:** counterfeiting.

731. **in . . . heaven's despite:** to spite heaven.

733. **Destinies:** the classical Fates.

734. **cross:** impair; **curious:** skillful; exquisite.

736. **defeature:** defect.

737. **tyranny:** violent action.

739. **agues pale and faint:** fevers, causing pallor and faintness.

740. **wood:** mad.

741. **attaint:** infection.

743. **imposthumes:** abscesses.

744. **Swear Nature's death:** vow nature's destruction.

"I am," quoth he, "expected of my friends;
And now 'tis dark, and going I shall fall."
"In night," quoth she, "desire sees best of all.   720

"But if thou fall, O, then imagine this,
The earth, in love with thee, thy footing trips,
And all is but to rob thee of a kiss.
Rich preys make true men thieves; so do thy lips
    Make modest Dian cloudy and forlorn,   725
    Lest she should steal a kiss, and die forsworn.

"Now of this dark night I perceive the reason:
Cynthia for shame obscures her silver shine,
Till forging Nature be condemned of treason,
For stealing molds from heaven that were divine,   730
    Wherein she framed thee, in high heaven's despite,
    To shame the sun by day and her by night.

"And therefore hath she bribed the Destinies
To cross the curious workmanship of Nature,
To mingle beauty with infirmities   735
And pure perfection with impure defeature,
    Making it subject to the tyranny
    Of mad mischances and much misery;

"As burning fevers, agues pale and faint,
Life-poisoning pestilence and frenzies wood,   740
The marrow-eating sickness whose attaint
Disorder breeds by heating of the blood,
    Surfeits, imposthumes, grief and damned despair,
    Swear Nature's death for framing thee so fair.

747. **favor:** facial appearance; **hue:** complexion or shape.
748. **late:** recently.
749. **done:** destroyed.
751. **despite of:** in defiance of.
752. **vestals:** vestal virgins.
762. **Sith:** since.
763. **made away:** killed.
764. **mischief:** evil.
766. **reaves:** bereaves.
767. **frets:** wears.
768. **put to use:** loaned out at interest.

"And not the least of all these maladies   745
But in one minute's fight brings beauty under.
Both favor, savor, hue and qualities,
Whereat th'impartial gazer late did wonder,
  Are on the sudden wasted, thawed and done,
  As mountain snow melts with the midday sun.   750

"Therefore, despite of fruitless chastity,
Love-lacking vestals and self-loving nuns,
That on the earth would breed a scarcity
And barren dearth of daughters and of sons,
  Be prodigal: the lamp that burns by night   755
  Dries up his oil to lend the world his light.

"What is thy body but a swallowing grave,
Seeming to bury that posterity
Which by the rights of time thou needs must have,
If thou destroy them not in dark obscurity?   760
  If so, the world will hold thee in disdain,
  Sith in thy pride so fair a hope is slain.

"So in thyself thyself art made away;
A mischief worse than civil home-bred strife,
Or theirs whose desperate hands themselves do slay,   765
Or butcher sire that reaves his son of life.
  Foul cank'ring rust the hidden treasure frets,
  But gold that's put to use more gold begets."

"Nay, then," quoth Adon, "you will fall again
Into your idle over-handled theme;   770
The kiss I gave you is bestowed in vain,

773. **foul:** ugly.
782. **closure:** enclosure.
787. **urged:** mentioned; **reprove:** refute.
789. **device:** strategy.
791. **increase:** procreation.
792. **bawd:** go-between.
795. **simple semblance:** innocent look.
797. **bereaves:** takes away.

"Bewitching like the wanton mermaid's songs"
The emblem shows Ulysses tied to his mast so he could not pursue
the mermaids, or sirens, to his and his ship's destruction. From
Whitney's *A Choice of Emblems* (1586).

And all in vain you strive against the stream;
 For, by this black-faced night, desire's foul nurse,
 Your treatise makes me like you worse and worse.

"If love have lent you twenty thousand tongues, 775
And every tongue more moving than your own,
Bewitching like the wanton mermaid's songs,
Yet from mine ear the tempting tune is blown;
 For know, my heart stands armed in mine ear,
 And will not let a false sound enter there, 780

"Lest the deceiving harmony should run
Into the quiet closure of my breast;
And then my little heart were quite undone,
In his bedchamber to be barred of rest.
 No, lady, no; my heart longs not to groan, 785
 But soundly sleeps, while now it sleeps alone.

"What have you urged that I cannot reprove?
The path is smooth that leadeth on to danger;
I hate not love, but your device in love
That lends embracements unto every stranger. 790
 You do it for increase: O strange excuse,
 When reason is the bawd to lust's abuse!

"Call it not love, for Love to heaven is fled
Since sweating Lust on earth usurped his name;
Under whose simple semblance he hath fed 795
Upon fresh beauty, blotting it with blame;
 Which the hot tyrant stains and soon bereaves,
 As caterpillars do the tender leaves.

806. **green:** inexperienced.
807. **sadness:** earnest.
808. **teen:** distress; grief.
813. **laund:** open pasture land.
821. **pitchy:** black.
825. **'stonished:** confused.

"Look how a bright star shooteth from the sky"
A comet. From Conrad Lycosthenes, *Prodigiorum ac ostentorum chronicon* (1557).

"Love comforteth like sunshine after rain,
But Lust's effect is tempest after sun;   800
Love's gentle spring doth always fresh remain,
Lust's winter comes ere summer half be done;
    Love surfeits not, Lust like a glutton dies;
    Love is all truth, Lust full of forged lies.

"More I could tell, but more I dare not say;   805
The text is old, the orator too green.
Therefore, in sadness, now I will away;
My face is full of shame, my heart of teen:
    Mine ears that to your wanton talk attended
    Do burn themselves for having so offended."   810

With this, he breaketh from the sweet embrace
Of those fair arms which bound him to her breast,
And homeward through the dark laund runs apace;
Leaves Love upon her back deeply distressed.
    Look how a bright star shooteth from the sky,   815
    So glides he in the night from Venus' eye;

Which after him she darts, as one on shore
Gazing upon a late-embarked friend,
Till the wild waves will have him seen no more,
Whose ridges with the meeting clouds contend;   820
    So did the merciless and pitchy night
    Fold in the object that did feed her sight.

Whereat amazed as one that unaware
Hath dropped a precious jewel in the flood,
Or 'stonished as night-wand'rers often are,   825

826. **mistrustful:** untrustworthy.

828. **the fair discovery of her way:** i.e., the beautiful Adonis, light of her life.

832. **Passion:** lament; **deeply:** i.e., in bass tones, or perhaps within the depths of the caves mentioned, or profoundly.

837. **thrall:** captive.

839. **heavy:** sorrowful.

841. **outwore:** outlasted.

844. **circumstance:** ceremony.

848. **parasites:** yes men.

849. **tapsters:** see *1 Henry IV*, II. iv, for the teasing of Francis the tapster by Prince Hal and Poins.

Their light blown out in some mistrustful wood;
  Even so confounded in the dark she lay,
  Having lost the fair discovery of her way.

And now she beats her heart, whereat it groans,
That all the neighbor caves, as seeming troubled,   830
Make verbal repetition of her moans;
Passion on passion deeply is redoubled:
  "Ay me!" she cries, and twenty times, "Woe, woe!"
  And twenty echoes twenty times cry so.

She, marking them, begins a wailing note,   835
And sings extemporally a woeful ditty;
How love makes young men thrall, and old men dote;
How love is wise in folly, foolish witty:
  Her heavy anthem still concludes in woe,
  And still the choir of echoes answer so.   840

Her song was tedious, and outwore the night,
For lovers' hours are long, though seeming short;
If pleased themselves, others, they think, delight
In such-like circumstance, with such-like sport.
  Their copious stories, oftentimes begun,   845
  End without audience, and are never done.

For who hath she to spend the night withal
But idle sounds resembling parasites,
Like shrill-tongued tapsters answering every call,
Soothing the humor of fantastic wits?   850
  She says "'Tis so"; they answer all "'Tis so";
  And would say after her, if she said "No."

854. **moist cabinet:** dewy abode.

857. **gloriously behold:** i.e., look down upon and gloriously illumine.

860. **clear:** shining.

866. **Musing:** wondering; **o'erworn:** spent.

870. **coasteth:** i.e., moves toward the sound, shifting direction as necessary.

874. **strict:** closely confining.

877. **at a bay:** holding the quarry at bay.

"She hearkens for his hounds and for his horn"
A huntsman. From Hartman Schopper, Πανοπλια *omnium* (1568).

Lo, here the gentle lark, weary of rest,
From his moist cabinet mounts up on high,
And wakes the morning, from whose silver breast   855
The sun ariseth in his majesty;
　　Who doth the world so gloriously behold
　　That cedar-tops and hills seem burnished gold.

Venus salutes him with this fair good-morrow:
"O thou clear god, and patron of all light,   860
From whom each lamp and shining star doth borrow
The beauteous influence that makes him bright,
　　There lives a son that sucked an earthly mother
　　May lend thee light, as thou dost lend to other."

This said, she hasteth to a myrtle grove,   865
Musing the morning is so much o'erworn,
And yet she hears no tidings of her love;
She hearkens for his hounds and for his horn.
　　Anon she hears them chant it lustily,
　　And all in haste she coasteth to the cry.   870

And as she runs, the bushes in the way
Some catch her by the neck, some kiss her face,
Some twind about her thigh to make her stay;
She wildly breaketh from their strict embrace,
　　Like a milch doe, whose swelling dugs do ache,   875
　　Hasting to feed her fawn hid in some brake.

By this she hears the hounds are at a bay;
Whereat she starts, like one that spies an adder
Wreathed up in fatal folds just in his way,

884. **blunt:** merciless; **proud:** spirited.

887. **curst:** truculent.

888. **strain court'sy who shall cope him first:** i.e., hang back politely to allow another to make the first assault on the quarry.

889. **dismal:** ill-omened; **sadly:** so as to cause grief.

890. **surprise:** master.

891. **bloodless fear:** i.e., fear that causes blood to drain from the heart.

893. **yield:** run.

894. **stay the field:** see the battle out.

895. **trembling ecstasy:** fit of trembling.

897. **causeless fantasy:** baseless fancy.

906. **rate:** berate; reproach.

The fear whereof doth make him shake and shudder; 880
  Even so the timorous yelping of the hounds
  Appalls her senses and her spirit confounds.

For now she knows it is no gentle chase,
But the blunt boar, rough bear, or lion proud,
Because the cry remaineth in one place, 885
Where fearfully the dogs exclaim aloud.
  Finding their enemy to be so curst,
  They all strain court'sy who shall cope him first.

This dismal cry rings sadly in her ear,
Through which it enters to surprise her heart; 890
Who, overcome by doubt and bloodless fear,
With cold-pale weakness numbs each feeling part;
  Like soldiers, when their captain once doth yield,
  They basely fly and dare not stay the field.

Thus stands she in a trembling ecstasy; 895
Till, cheering up her senses all dismayed,
She tells them 'tis a causeless fantasy,
And childish error, that they are afraid;
  Bids them leave quaking, bids them fear no more;
  And with that word she spied the hunted boar, 900

Whose frothy mouth, bepainted all with red,
Like milk and blood being mingled both together,
A second fear through all her sinews spread,
Which madly hurries her she knows not whither:
  This way she runs, and now she will no further, 905
  But back retires to rate the boar for murther.

907. **spleens:** violent emotions.

908. **untreads again:** retraces.

909. **mated:** frustrated; offset.

911. **Full of respects, yet nought at all respecting:** i.e., preoccupied with many flashing thoughts, none of which she dwells on.

912. **In hand with all things, nought at all effecting:** proposing to do everything but doing nothing.

914. **caitiff:** wretch.

916. **sovereign:** paramount.

920. **flap-mouthed:** loose-jowled.

921. **welkin:** sky.

925. **Look how:** just as.

926. **prodigies:** extraordinary phenomena; marvels.

930. **exclaims on:** rails at.

931. **Hard-favored:** ugly; ill-featured; **meager:** emaciated.

933. **worm:** possibly cankerworm, which causes destruction.

A thousand spleens bear her a thousand ways;
She treads the path that she untreads again;
Her more than haste is mated with delays,
Like the proceedings of a drunken brain,   910
  Full of respects, yet nought at all respecting,
  In hand with all things, nought at all effecting.

Here kennelled in a brake she finds a hound,
And asks the weary caitiff for his master;
And there another licking of his wound,   915
'Gainst venomed sores the only sovereign plaster;
  And here she meets another sadly scowling,
  To whom she speaks, and he replies with howling.

When he hath ceased his ill-resounding noise,
Another flap-mouthed mourner, black and grim,   920
Against the welkin volleys out his voice;
Another and another answer him,
  Clapping their proud tails to the ground below,
  Shaking their scratched ears, bleeding as they go.

Look how the world's poor people are amazed   925
At apparitions, signs and prodigies,
Whereon with fearful eyes they long have gazed,
Infusing them with dreadful prophecies;
  So she at these sad signs draws up her breath,
  And, sighing it again, exclaims on Death.   930

"Hard-favored tyrant, ugly, meager, lean,
Hateful divorce of love"—thus chides she Death—
"Grim-grinning host, earth's worm, what dost thou
      mean

936. **Gloss:** beauty; brilliance.

940. **randon:** variant of random.

941. **false:** acting contrary to right.

947. **Love's golden arrow:** the golden arrow by which Cupid was reputed to cause love. For the tale of the exchange of darts between Love and Death see the cut and accompanying rhyme.

949. **Dost thou drink tears, that thou provokest such weeping:** i.e., do you cause such weeping because of your thirst for tears.

953. **cares not for:** is unconcerned about; **mortal vigor:** deadly power.

956. **vailed:** lowered; **sluices:** floodgates.

WHILE furious Mors, from place, to place did flie,
And here, and there, her fatall dartes did throwe:
At lengthe shee mette, with Cupid passing by,
Who likewise had, bene busie with his bowe:
Within one Inne, they bothe togeather stay'd,
And for one nighte, awaie theire shooting layd.

The morrowe next, they bothe awaie doe haste,
And eache by chaunce, the others quiuer takes:
The frozen dartes, on Cupiddes backe weare plac'd,
The fierie dartes, the leane virago shakes:
Whereby ensued, suche alteration straunge,
As all the worlde, did wonder at the chaunge.

For gallant youthes, whome Cupid thoughte to wounde,
Of loue, and life, did make an ende at once.
And aged men, whome deathe woulde bringe to grounde:
Beganne againe to loue, with sighes, and grones:
Thus natures lawes, this chaunce infringed soe:
That age did loue, and youthe to graue did goe.

Exchange of darts between Love and Death. From Whitney's *A Choice of Emblems* (1586).

To stifle beauty and to steal his breath
  Who when he lived, his breath and beauty set   935
  Gloss on the rose, smell to the violet?

"If he be dead—O no, it cannot be,
Seeing his beauty, thou shouldst strike at it—
O yes, it may; thou hast no eyes to see,
But hatefully at randon dost thou hit.   940
  Thy mark is feeble age; but thy false dart
  Mistakes that aim, and cleaves an infant's heart.

"Hadst thou but bid beware, then he had spoke,
And, hearing him, thy power had lost his power.
The Destinies will curse thee for this stroke;   945
They bid thee crop a weed, thou pluck'st a flower.
  Love's golden arrow at him should have fled,
  And not Death's ebon dart, to strike him dead.

"Dost thou drink tears, that thou provokest such
    weeping?
What may a heavy groan advantage thee?   950
Why hast thou cast into eternal sleeping
Those eyes that taught all other eyes to see?
  Now Nature cares not for thy mortal vigor,
  Since her best work is ruined with thy rigor."

Here overcome as one full of despair,   955
She vailed her eyelids, who, like sluices, stopped
The crystal tide that from her two cheeks fair
In the sweet channel of her bosom dropped;
  But through the floodgates breaks the silver rain,
  And with his strong course opens them again.   960

967. **throng:** beset, like suitors.

969. **entertained:** welcomed.

972. **consulting:** plotting.

975. **dire imagination she did follow:** woeful train of thought she pursued.

978. **flatters:** fosters hope that.

981. **orient:** lustrous.

984. **she:** i.e., the ground, likened to a sluttish woman.

985-86. **how strange it seems/ Not to believe:** how aloof it seems in disbelieving; how reluctant it is to believe.

987. **weal:** sorrow.

O, how her eyes and tears did lend and borrow!
Her eye seen in the tears, tears in her eye;
Both crystals, where they viewed each other's sorrow,
Sorrow that friendly sighs sought still to dry;
   But like a stormy day, now wind, now rain,   965
   Sighs dry her cheeks, tears make them wet again.

Variable passions throng her constant woe,
As striving who should best become her grief;
All entertained, each passion labors so
That every present sorrow seemeth chief,   970
   But none is best. Then join they all together,
   Like many clouds consulting for foul weather.

By this, far off she hears some huntsman holla;
A nurse's song ne'er pleased her babe so well.
The dire imagination she did follow   975
This sound of hope doth labor to expel;
   For now reviving joy bids her rejoice,
   And flatters her it is Adonis' voice.

Whereat her tears began to turn their tide,
Being prisoned in her eye like pearls in glass;   980
Yet sometimes falls an orient drop beside,
Which her cheek melts, as scorning it should pass
   To wash the foul face of the sluttish ground,
   Who is but drunken when she seemeth drowned.

O hard-believing love, how strange it seems   985
Not to believe, and yet too credulous!
Thy weal and woe are both of them extremes;

989. **The one:** hope.

990. **kills thee:** i.e., in the thought that Adonis is really dead. Love's behavior is absurd, according to the conceit here, because *likely* can mean "hopeful," as well as meaning "probable."

991. **unweaves the web that she hath wrought:** perhaps echoing Penelope's ruse of unweaving the work she had done on the robe she was supposedly making for Laertes, her father-in-law (*Odyssey*, bk. ii).

992. **to blame:** blameworthy.

993. **all to nought:** thoroughly wicked.

995. **clepes:** calls.

1000. **still severe:** always merciless.

1001. **gentle:** courteous.

1002. **railed:** scolded.

1004. **wreaked:** revenged.

1006. **author:** instigator.

1010. **suspect:** suspicion; **extenuate:** excuse.

1012. **insinuate:** flatter.

1013. **stories:** relates.

Jove, king of the gods, with his thunderbolts. From Cartari's *Imagini* (1615).

Despair, and hope, makes thee ridiculous:
  The one doth flatter thee in thoughts unlikely,
  In likely thoughts the other kills thee quickly.   990

Now she unweaves the web that she hath wrought;
Adonis lives, and Death is not to blame;
It was not she that called him all to nought.
Now she adds honors to his hateful name;
  She clepes him king of graves, and grave for kings, 995
  Imperious supreme of all mortal things.

"No, no," quoth she, "sweet Death, I did but jest;
Yet pardon me, I felt a kind of fear
When as I met the boar, that bloody beast,
Which knows no pity, but is still severe.   1000
  Then, gentle shadow—truth I must confess—
  I railed on thee, fearing my love's decease.

"'Tis not my fault: the boar provoked my tongue;
Be wreaked on him, invisible commander;
'Tis he, foul creature, that hath done thee wrong; 1005
I did but act, he's author of thy slander.
  Grief hath two tongues, and never woman yet
  Could rule them both without ten women's wit."

Thus, hoping that Adonis is alive,
Her rash suspect she doth extenuate;   1010
And that his beauty may the better thrive,
With Death she humbly doth insinuate;
  Tells him of trophies, statues, tombs, and stories
  His victories, his triumphs and his glories.

1018. **mutual:** common.

1023. **unwitnessed with:** unattested by.

1024. **grieves:** grieves for.

1026. **leaps:** bounds joyfully.

1027. **lure:** a decoy bird, made of feathers to which some flesh was attached to lure the falcon.

1028. **stoops:** bends.

1032. **ashamed of:** put to shame by.

1039. **office:** function.

1040. **disposing:** disposition; control.

1041. **consort:** associate.

"And, beauty dead, black chaos comes again."
A conception of chaos from Whitney's
A Choice of Emblems (1586).

"O Jove," quoth she, "how much a fool was I   1015
To be of such a weak and silly mind
To wail his death who lives and must not die
Till mutual overthrow of mortal kind!
　For he being dead, with him is beauty slain,
　And, beauty dead, black chaos comes again.   1020

"Fie, fie, fond love, thou art as full of fear
As one with treasure laden, hemmed with thieves;
Trifles unwitnessed with eye or ear
Thy coward heart with false bethinking grieves."
　Even at this word she hears a merry horn,   1025
　Whereat she leaps that was but late forlorn.

As falcons to the lure, away she flies;
The grass stoops not, she treads on it so light;
And in her haste unfortunately spies
The foul boar's conquest on her fair delight;   1030
　Which seen, her eyes, as murdered with the view,
　Like stars ashamed of day, themselves withdrew;

Or as the snail, whose tender horns being hit,
Shrinks backward in his shelly cave with pain,
And there all smothered up in shade doth sit,   1035
Long after fearing to creep forth again;
　So at his bloody view her eyes are fled
　Into the deep-dark cabins of her head;

Where they resign their office and their light
To the disposing of her troubled brain;   1040
Who bids them still consort with ugly night,

1043-45. Who, like a king perplexed . . . subject quakes: Cf. *King Lear* (IV, vi): "Ay, every inch a king! When I do stare, see how the subject quakes."

1046-47. wind . . . shakes: A reference to an ancient belief, found in Aristotle and Pliny, that winds deep in the earth caused earthquakes. An earthquake in 1580 made a lasting impression on Englishmen.

1048. confound: confuse.

1052. trenched: furrowed.

1054. purple: bright red; the word purple was frequently used to mean brilliant color, usually red.

1059. passions: mourns; **franticly she doteth:** she grieves deliriously.

1062. Her eyes . . . till now: Since she has so much to weep for now, her eyes reproach themselves for having wept before.

1064. sight dazzling . . . seem three: Cf. *3 Henry VI* (II, i): "Dazzle mine eyes, or do I see three suns?"

1065. reprehends: reproves; **mangling eye:** eye that makes the wound seem even worse than it is.

1066. breach: slash.

And never wound the heart with looks again;
  Who, like a king perplexed in his throne,
  By their suggestion gives a deadly groan,

Whereat each tributary subject quakes;   1045
As when the wind, imprisoned in the ground,
Struggling for passage, earth's foundation shakes,
Which with cold terror doth men's minds confound.
  This mutiny each part doth so surprise,
  That from their dark beds once more leap her eyes; 1050

And being opened, threw unwilling light
Upon the wide wound that the boar had trenched
In his soft flank; whose wonted lily white
With purple tears that his wound wept was drenched:
  No flower was nigh, no grass, herb, leaf or weed, 1055
  But stole his blood and seemed with him to bleed.

This solemn sympathy poor Venus noteth;
Over one shoulder doth she hang her head;
Dumbly she passions, franticly she doteth;
She thinks he could not die, he is not dead.   1060
  Her voice is stopped, her joints forget to bow;
  Her eyes are mad that they have wept till now.

Upon his hurt she looks so steadfastly
That her sight dazzling makes the wound seem three;
And then she reprehends her mangling eye   1065
That makes more gashes where no breach should be:
  His face seems twain, each several limb is doubled;
  For oft the eye mistakes, the brain being troubled.

1078. **ensuing:** in the future.
1083. **fair:** beauty.
1088. **gaudy:** brilliant.
1094. **fear him:** terrify him.

"My tongue cannot express my grief for one,
And yet," quoth she, "behold two Adons dead!   1070
My sighs are blown away, my salt tears gone,
Mine eyes are turned to fire, my heart to lead;
    Heavy heart's lead, melt at mine eyes' red fire!
    So shall I die by drops of hot desire.

"Alas, poor world, what treasure hast thou lost!   1075
What face remains alive that's worth the viewing?
Whose tongue is music now? What canst thou boast
Of things long since, or any thing ensuing?
    The flowers are sweet, their colors fresh and trim;
    But true sweet beauty lived and died with him.   1080

"Bonnet nor veil henceforth no creature wear;
Nor sun nor wind will ever strive to kiss you.
Having no fair to lose, you need not fear;
The sun doth scorn you, and the wind doth hiss you.
    But when Adonis lived, sun and sharp air   1085
    Lurked like two thieves to rob him of his fair;

"And therefore would he put his bonnet on,
Under whose brim the gaudy sun would peep;
The wind would blow it off, and, being gone,
Play with his locks. Then would Adonis weep;   1090
    And straight, in pity of his tender years,
    They both would strive who first should dry his
        tears.

"To see his face the lion walked along
Behind some hedge, because he would not fear him;
To recreate himself when he hath song,   1095

1105. **urchin-snouted:** urchin was a word for hedgehog; with a snout like a hedgehog's.

1106. **downward eye:** eye looking toward the earth.

1107. **livery:** external form that was his.

1108. **entertainment:** treatment.

1110. **He thought . . . killed him so:** Venus in her grief imagines that the boar must have tried to kiss Adonis and accidentally gored him, a conceit that goes back to Theocritus.

1113. **whet:** gnashed.

"He ran upon the boar with his sharp spear"
From Guillaume de La Perrière, *La morosophie* (1553).

44

The tiger would be tame and gently hear him;
    If he had spoke, the wolf would leave his prey,
    And never fright the silly lamb that day.

"When he beheld his shadow in the brook,
The fishes spread on it their golden gills;   1100
When he was by, the birds such pleasure took
That some would sing, some other in their bills
    Would bring him mulberries and ripe-red cherries;
    He fed them with his sight, they him with berries.

"But this foul, grim, and urchin-snouted boar,   1105
Whose downward eye still looketh for a grave,
Ne'er saw the beauteous livery that he wore;
Witness the entertainment that he gave.
    If he did see his face, why then I know
    He thought to kiss him, and hath killed him so.   1110

" 'Tis true, 'tis true; thus was Adonis slain:
He ran upon the boar with his sharp spear,
Who did not whet his teeth at him again,
But by a kiss thought to persuade him there;
    And nuzzling in his flank, the loving swine   1115
    Sheathed unaware the tusk in his soft groin.

"Had I been toothed like him, I must confess,
With kissing him I should have killed him first;
But he is dead, and never did he bless
My youth with his; the more am I accurst."   1120
    With this, she falleth in the place she stood,
    And stains her face with his congealed blood.

1127. **coffer-lids:** tops to treasure chests.

1133. **spite:** misfortune.

1142. **breathing while:** in the time required to take a breath.

1143. **o'erstrawed:** scattered over.

1144. **beguile:** deceive.

1148. **tread the measures:** dance.

1149. **staring:** furious.

Death of Adonis. From Alciati, *Omnia . . . emblemata* (1577).

She looks upon his lips, and they are pale;
She takes him by the hand, and that is cold;
She whispers in his ears a heavy tale,   1125
As if they heard the woeful words she told;
   She lifts the coffer-lids that close his eyes,
   Where, lo, two lamps, burnt out, in darkness lies;

Two glasses, where herself herself beheld
A thousand times, and now no more, reflect;   1130
Their virtue lost wherein they late excelled,
And every beauty robbed of his effect.
   "Wonder of time," quoth she, "this is my spite,
   That, thou being dead, the day should yet be light.

"Since thou art dead, lo, here I prophesy   1135
Sorrow on love hereafter shall attend;
It shall be waited on with jealousy,
Find sweet beginning but unsavory end;
   Ne'er settled equally, but high or low,
   That all love's pleasure shall not match his woe.   1140

"It shall be fickle, false and full of fraud;
Bud, and be blasted, in a breathing while;
The bottom poison, and the top o'erstrawed
With sweets that shall the truest sight beguile;
   The strongest body shall it make most weak,   1145
   Strike the wise dumb, and teach the fool to speak.

"It shall be sparing, and too full of riot,
Teaching decrepit age to tread the measures;
The staring ruffian shall it keep in quiet,

1157. **toward:** willing.

1168. **purple flower:** bright flower unnamed but in Ovid it is the anemone; **check'red:** spotted.

1174. **reft:** snatched.

An anemone, the flower that, by tradition, sprang from Adonis' blood. From Theophrastus, *De historia plantarum* (1644).

46

Pluck down the rich, enrich the poor with treasures;   1150
  It shall be raging-mad, and silly-mild,
  Make the young old, the old become a child.

"It shall suspect where is no cause of fear;
It shall not fear where it should most mistrust;
It shall be merciful and too severe,   1155
And most deceiving when it seems most just;
  Perverse it shall be where it shows most toward,
  Put fear to valor, courage to the coward.

"It shall be cause of war and dire events,
And set dissension 'twixt the son and sire;   1160
Subject and servile to all discontents,
As dry combustious matter is to fire.
  Sith in his prime death doth my love destroy,
  They that love best their loves shall not enjoy."

By this the boy that by her side lay killed   1165
Was melted like a vapor from her sight,
And in his blood that on the ground lay spilled
A purple flower sprung up, check'red with white,
  Resembling well his pale cheeks, and the blood
  Which in round drops upon their whiteness stood. 1170

She bows her head the new-sprung flower to smell,
Comparing it to her Adonis' breath;
And says within her bosom it shall dwell,
Since he himself is reft from her by death;
  She crops the stalk, and in the breach appears   1175
  Green-dropping sap, which she compares to tears.

1189. **hies:** flees.

1190. **yokes:** harnesses.

1193. **Paphos:** Ancient city on Cyprus, the site of a temple to Aphrodite, or Venus.

1194. **immure:** shut up.

Venus takes leave of Adonis and, "weary of the world," mounts her chariot for Paphos. From Ovid, *Metamorphoses* (ca. 1591).

"Poor flower," quoth she, "this was thy father's guise—
Sweet issue of a more sweet-smelling sire—
For every little grief to wet his eyes.
To grow unto himself was his desire,   1180
  And so 'tis thine; but know, it is as good
  To wither in my breast as in his blood.

"Here was thy father's bed, here in my breast;
Thou art the next of blood, and 'tis thy right.
Lo, in this hollow cradle take thy rest;   1185
My throbbing heart shall rock thee day and night;
  There shall not be one minute in an hour
  Wherein I will not kiss my sweet love's flower."

Thus weary of the world, away she hies,
And yokes her silver doves, by whose swift aid   1190
Their mistress, mounted, through the empty skies
In her light chariot quickly is conveyed,
  Holding their course to Paphos, where their queen
  Means to immure herself and not be seen.

THE RAPE OF LUCRECE

The tone of the dedication suggests that the poet had received from his patron some marked evidence of his favor. Southampton had evidently rewarded him with a generous gift. The warmth of the dedication, however, should not be interpreted too literally because extravagant language of this type, addressed to a would-be patron, was conventional in this age.

|||||||||||||||||||||||||||||||||||||||||

pamphlet without beginning: the reader is plunged into the midst of the story at once.

moiety: portion, not literally half.

TO THE

RIGHT HONORABLE
HENRY WRIOTHESLEY,

EARL OF SOUTHAMPTON, AND BARON
OF TITCHFIELD

The love I dedicate to your lordship is without end: whereof this pamphlet without beginning is but a superfluous moiety. The warrant I have of your honorable disposition, not the worth of my untutored lines, makes it assured of acceptance. What I have done is yours; what I have to do is yours; being part in all I have, devoted yours. Were my worth greater, my duty would show greater; meantime, as it is, it is bound to your lordship, to whom I wish long life still lengthened with all happiness.

Your lordship's in all duty,
William Shakespeare

The "Argument" is a brief summary of the story that Shakespeare proposes to tell in verse. The "Argument" mentions two messengers sent to Rome by Lucrece, but the poem reports only one. Such slight discrepancies have caused a few scholars to suggest that the "Argument" was supplied by someone other than the poet, but this conjecture seems unlikely.

▪▪▪▪▪▪▪▪▪▪▪▪▪▪▪▪▪▪▪▪▪▪▪▪▪▪▪▪▪▪▪▪▪▪

Lucius Tarquinius: the last of the legendary kings of Rome; he is reported to have ruled from 534 to 510 B.C.

Ardea: a town a little more than twenty miles south of Rome.

Collatium: a town some ten miles east of Rome.

THE ARGUMENT

LUCIUS TARQUINIUS, for his excessive pride surnamed
Superbus, after he had caused his own father-in-law
Servius Tullius to be cruelly murdered, and, contrary
to the Roman laws and customs, not requiring or
staying for the people's suffrages, had possessed himself of the kingdom, went, accompanied with his sons
and other noblemen of Rome, to besiege Ardea. During which siege the principal men of the army meeting one evening at the tent of Sextus Tarquinius, the
king's son, in their discourses after supper every one
commended the virtues of his own wife; among
whom Collatinus extolled the incomparable chastity
of his wife Lucretia. In that pleasant humor they all
posted to Rome; and intending, by their secret and
sudden arrival, to make trial of that which every one
had before avouched, only Collatinus finds his wife,
though it were late in the night, spinning amongst
her maids: the other ladies were all found dancing
and reveling, or in several disports. Whereupon the
noblemen yielded Collatinus the victory, and his wife
the fame. At that time Sextus Tarquinius being in-
flamed with Lucrece' beauty, yet smothering his

The frontispiece to the 1655 edition of *The Rape of Lucrece*.

passions for the present, departed with the rest back to the camp; from whence he shortly after privily withdrew himself, and was, according to his estate, royally entertained and lodged by Lucrece at Collatium. The same night he treacherously stealeth into her chamber, violently ravished her, and early in the morning speedeth away. Lucrece, in this lamentable plight, hastily dispatcheth messengers, one to Rome for her father, another to the camp for Collatine. They came, the one accompanied with Junius Brutus, the other with Publius Valerius; and finding Lucrece attired in mourning habit, demanded the cause of her sorrow. She, first taking an oath of them for her revenge, revealed the actor and whole manner of his dealing, and withal suddenly stabbed herself. Which done, with one consent they all vowed to root out the whole hated family of the Tarquins; and bearing the dead body to Rome, Brutus acquainted the people with the doer and manner of the vile deed, with a bitter invective against the tyranny of the king: wherewith the people were so moved, that with one consent and a general acclamation the Tarquins were all exiled, and the state government changed from kings to consuls.

The verse form of *Lucrece* is a seven-line stanza, rhyming *ab ab b cc*, known as rhyme royal, a stanza long popular in English poetry.

▪▪▪▪▪▪▪▪▪▪▪▪▪▪▪▪▪▪▪▪▪▪▪▪▪▪▪▪▪▪▪▪

1. **in post:** with the speed of a postrider or mail carrier.

2. **trustless:** faithless.

4. **lightless:** smouldering.

8. **Haply:** by chance.

9. **bateless:** unblunted; keen.

10. **let:** forbear.

14. **aspects:** influence of the planets; **peculiar:** special.

A Roman camp, such as the one at Ardea, as imagined in Elizabethan England. From Raphael Holinshed, *Chronicles* (1577).

THE RAPE OF LUCRECE

From the besieged Ardea all in post,
Borne by the trustless wings of false desire,
Lust-breathed Tarquin leaves the Roman host,
And to Collatium bears the lightless fire
Which, in pale embers hid, lurks to aspire   5
   And girdle with embracing flames the waist
   Of Collatine's fair love, Lucrece the chaste.

Haply that name of chaste unhapp'ly set
This bateless edge on his keen appetite;
When Collatine unwisely did not let   10
To praise the clear unmatched red and white
Which triumphed in that sky of his delight,
   Where mortal stars, as bright as heaven's beauties,
   With pure aspects did him peculiar duties.

For he the night before, in Tarquin's tent,   15
Unlocked the treasure of his happy state;
What priceless wealth the heavens had him lent
In the possession of his beauteous mate;
Reck'ning his fortune at such high-proud rate
   That kings might be espoused to more fame,   20
   But king nor peer to such a peerless dame.

32. **singular:** without an equal.

36. **sov'reignty:** superiority.

37. **Suggested:** stirred up; **issue:** offspring.

38. **tainted:** corrupted.

42. **hap:** chance.

47. **liver:** the seat of passion was believed to be the liver.

48-49. **O rash-false heat . . . grows old:** this treacherous lust will bring cold repentance, like the blasts that blight an early spring.

a) A Roman patrician of the time of Tarquin.
b) A Roman lady of the general appearance of Lucrece.
Both from Cesare Vecellio, *Habiti antichi et moderni di tutto il mondo* (1590).

O happiness enjoyed but of a few!
And, if possessed, as soon decayed and done
As is the morning silver-melting dew
Against the golden splendor of the sun!   25
An expired date, canceled ere well begun:
  Honor and beauty, in the owner's arms,
  Are weakly fortressed from a world of harms.

Beauty itself doth of itself persuade
The eyes of men without an orator;   30
What needeth then apology be made,
To set forth that which is so singular?
Or why is Collatine the publisher
  Of that rich jewel he should keep unknown
  From thievish ears, because it is his own?   35

Perchance his boast of Lucrece' sov'reignty
Suggested this proud issue of a king;
For by our ears our hearts oft tainted be.
Perchance that envy of so rich a thing,
Braving compare, disdainfully did sting   40
  His high-pitched thoughts, that meaner men
    should vaunt
  That golden hap which their superiors want.

But some untimely thought did instigate
His all too timeless speed, if none of those.
His honor, his affairs, his friends, his state,   45
Neglected all, with swift intent he goes
To quench the coal which in his liver glows.
  O rash-false heat, wrapped in repentant cold,
  Thy hasty spring still blasts, and ne'er grows old!

53. **underprop:** uphold; support.

55. **in despite:** in scorn.

57. **intituled:** had a right to.

58. **fair field:** Shakespeare compares Lucrece's face to a coat-of-arms.

63. **fence:** protect; the sense is that blushes stand guard over the white of innocence.

67. **world's minority:** early time.

69. **sovereignty:** power.

71. **silent war:** the contest between red and white in Lucrece's cheeks. This long-drawn-out metaphor suggests that Lucrece's fair looks take captive Tarquin's eye but would willingly let go so false an enemy.

VENUS.

Venus' doves drawing her chariot. From a woodcut in John Indagine, *The Book of Palmistry* (1666).

When at Collatium this false lord arrived,   50
Well was he welcomed by the Roman dame,
Within whose face beauty and virtue strived
Which of them both should underprop her fame:
When virtue bragged, beauty would blush for shame;
  When beauty boasted blushes, in despite   55
  Virtue would stain that o'er with silver white.

But beauty, in that white intituled,
From Venus' doves doth challenge that fair field;
Then virtue claims from beauty beauty's red,
Which virtue gave the golden age to gild   60
Their silver cheeks, and called it then their shield;
  Teaching them thus to use it in the fight,
  When shame assailed, the red should fence
    the white.

This heraldry in Lucrece' face was seen,
Argued by beauty's red and virtue's white;   65
Of either's color was the other queen,
Proving from world's minority their right;
Yet their ambition makes them still to fight,
  The sovereignty of either being so great
  That oft they interchange each other's seat.   70

This silent war of lilies and of roses
Which Tarquin viewed in her fair face's field,
In their pure ranks his traitor eye encloses;
Where, lest between them both it should be killed,
The coward captive vanquished doth yield   75
  To those two armies that would let him go
  Rather than triumph in so false a foe.

78. **shallow tongue:** thoughtless speech.

79. **niggard prodigal:** a rhetorical device called "oxymoron" that combines two contradictory and incongruous words. The sense is that the too-prodigal husband was actually niggardly in praise of Lucrece.

83. **answers with surmise:** responds with amazement (to Lucrece's beauty).

88. **Birds never limed:** birds never caught by the method of smearing twigs with a sticky substance.

90. **reverend:** respectful.

92. **colored with his high estate:** his princely position made him seem above reproach.

93. **pleats of majesty:** under cover of his princely dignity.

98. **cloyed:** glutted.

99. **coped with:** contended with.

100. **parling:** speaking.

102. **glassy margents . . . books:** the shining glint from his eyes.

104. **wanton:** lewd.

Now thinks he that her husband's shallow tongue,
The niggard prodigal that praised her so,
In that high task hath done her beauty wrong,   80
Which far exceeds his barren skill to show;
Therefore that praise which Collatine doth owe
  Enchanted Tarquin answers with surmise,
  In silent wonder of still-gazing eyes.

This earthly saint, adored by this devil,   85
Little suspecteth the false worshipper;
For unstained thoughts do seldom dream on evil;
Birds never limed no secret bushes fear.
So guiltless she securely gives good cheer
  And reverend welcome to her princely guest,   90
  Whose inward ill no outward harm expressed;

For that he colored with his high estate,
Hiding base sin in pleats of majesty;
That nothing in him seemed inordinate,
Save sometime too much wonder of his eye,   95
Which, having all, all could not satisfy;
  But, poorly rich, so wanteth in his store
  That cloyed with much he pineth still for more.

But she, that never coped with stranger eyes,
Could pick no meaning from their parling looks,   100
Nor read the subtle-shining secrecies
Writ in the glassy margents of such books.
She touched no unknown baits, nor feared no hooks;
  Nor could she moralize his wanton sight,
  More than his eyes were opened to the light.   105

106. **stories:** reports.

110. **bruised arms:** dinted armor.

111. **heaved-up:** lifted.

116. **welkin:** sky.

121. **Intending . . . sprite:** pretending to be weary and dull in spirit.

128. **will's:** desire's.

130. **weak-built hopes:** meaning that Tarquin has had no encouragement to think that he can gain his desires.

131. **Despair . . . gaining:** even when there is despair of profit, trade goes on.

132. **meed proposed:** gain anticipated.

A wreath of victory, made of oak leaves. Laurel was also frequently used by the ancients. From Claude Guichard, *Funerailles* (1581).

He stories to her ears her husband's fame,
Won in the fields of fruitful Italy;
And decks with praises Collatine's high name,
Made glorious by his manly chivalry
With bruised arms and wreaths of victory.   110
  Her joy with heaved-up hand she doth express,
  And wordless so greets heaven for his success.

Far from the purpose of his coming thither,
He makes excuses for his being there.
No cloudy show of stormy blust'ring weather   115
Doth yet in his fair welkin once appear;
Till sable Night, mother of dread and fear,
  Upon the world dim darkness doth display,
  And in her vaulty prison stows the day.

For then is Tarquin brought unto his bed,   120
Intending weariness with heavy sprite;
For after supper long he questioned
With modest Lucrece, and wore out the night.
Now leaden slumber with life's strength doth fight;
  And every one to rest himself betake,   125
  Save thieves and cares and troubled minds
      that wake.

As one of which doth Tarquin lie revolving
The sundry dangers of his will's obtaining;
Yet ever to obtain his will resolving,
Though weak-built hopes persuade him to abstaining;   130
Despair to gain doth traffic oft for gaining,
  And when great treasure is the meed proposed,

133. **adjunct:** associated with; this passage means that although the threat of death may be involved, one does not believe it.

134. **with gain so fond:** made foolish by gain.

135-37. **That what . . . but less:** the passage, boiled down, means that covetous people, seeking greater profits, often scatter and lose the gains they have in seeking more.

144. **gage:** pawn; venture.

145. **fell:** deadly.

155. **hazard:** chance.

157. **himself he must forsake:** he must abandon his better instincts.

Though death be adjunct, there's no death
   supposed.

Those that much covet are with gain so fond
That what they have not, that which they possess,   135
They scatter and unloose it from their bond,
And so, by hoping more, they have but less;
Or, gaining more, the profit of excess
   Is but to surfeit, and such griefs sustain
   That they prove bankrupt in this poor-rich gain.   140

The aim of all is but to nurse the life
With honor, wealth and ease, in waning age;
And in this aim there is such thwarting strife
That one for all or all for one we gage:
As life for honor in fell battle's rage;   145
   Honor for wealth; and oft that wealth doth cost
   The death of all, and all together lost.

So that in vent'ring ill we leave to be
The things we are for that which we expect;
And this ambitious foul infirmity,   150
In having much, torments us with defect
Of that we have; so then we do neglect
   The thing we have, and, all for want of wit,
   Make something nothing by augmenting it.

Such hazard now must doting Tarquin make,   155
Pawning his honor to obtain his lust;
And for himself himself he must forsake:
Then where is truth, if there be no self-trust?
When shall he think to find a stranger just

160. **confounds:** destroys.
164. **comfortable:** comforting.
165. **death-boding cries:** cries foretelling death.
167. **silly:** harmless.
176. **falchion:** sword.
179. **lodestar:** guide.
183. **premeditate:** think about.

"Now serves the season that they may surprise
The silly lambs. Pure thoughts are dead and still,
While lust and murder wakes to stain and kill."
From *Le microcosme, contenant divers tableaux* (Amsterdam, n.d.).

When he himself himself confounds, betrays   160
  To sland'rous tongues and wretched hateful days?

Now stole upon the time the dead of night,
When heavy sleep had closed up mortal eyes;
No comfortable star did lend his light,
No noise but owls' and wolves' death-boding cries;   165
Now serves the season that they may surprise
  The silly lambs. Pure thoughts are dead and still,
  While lust and murder wakes to stain and kill.

And now this lustful lord, leaped from his bed,
Throwing his mantle rudely o'er his arm,   170
Is madly tossed between desire and dread;
The one sweetly flatters, the other feareth harm;
But honest fear, bewitched with lust's foul charm,
  Doth too too oft betake him to retire,
  Beaten away by brain-sick rude desire.   175

His falchion on a flint he softly smiteth,
That from the cold stone sparks of fire do fly,
Whereat a waxen torch forthwith he lighteth,
Which must be lodestar to his lustful eye;
And to the flame thus speaks advisedly: 180
  "As from this cold flint I enforced this fire,
  So Lucrece must I force to my desire."

Here pale with fear he doth premeditate
The dangers of his loathsome enterprise,
And in his inward mind he doth debate   185
What following sorrow may on this arise;
Then, looking scornfully, he doth despise

188. **His naked . . . lust:** the meaning of this line has been a matter of scholarly conjecture; perhaps the line means that only lust is Tarquin's armor and that dies when it is satisfied.

196. **weed:** garment.

198. **household's grave:** burial place of his ancestors.

200. **martial man:** soldier; **fancy's:** love's or affection's.

202. **digression:** deviation from virtue.

205. **golden coat:** books of heraldry; escutcheon.

206. **dash:** mark of dishonor.

207. **cipher:** indicate; **fondly:** foolishly; **dote:** love to excess.

208. **posterity:** descendants.

212. **froth:** unsubstantial foam.

"O shame to knighthood and to shining arms!
. . . .
A martial man to be soft fancy's slave!"
A knight in armor. From an engraving by C. F. Tomkins after
J. R. Planché, *Costume Designs for Richard III* (1829).

His naked armor of still-slaughtered lust,
And justly thus controls his thoughts unjust:

"Fair torch, burn out thy light, and lend it not   190
To darken her whose light excelleth thine;
And die, unhallowed thoughts, before you blot
With your uncleanness that which is divine;
Offer pure incense to so pure a shrine;
    Let fair humanity abhor the deed   195
    That spots and stains love's modest snow-white
        weed.

"O shame to knighthood and to shining arms!
O foul dishonor to my household's grave!
O impious act, including all foul harms!
A martial man to be soft fancy's slave!   200
True valor still a true respect should have;
    Then my digression is so vile, so base,
    That it will live engraven in my face.

"Yea, though I die, the scandal will survive,
And be an eye-sore in my golden coat;   205
Some loathsome dash the herald will contrive,
To cipher me how fondly I did dote;
That my posterity, shamed with the note,
    Shall curse my bones, and hold it for no sin
    To wish that I their father had not been.   210

"What win I, if I gain the thing I seek?
A dream, a breath, a froth of fleeting joy.
Who buys a minute's mirth to wail a week?
Or sells eternity to get a toy?

217. **scepter:** baton; emblem of royal authority.
221. **engirt:** surrounded.
236. **quittal:** requital; retaliation.
239. **fact:** deed.
241. **not her own:** she belongs to her husband.

For one sweet grape who will the vine destroy?   215
  Or what fond beggar, but to touch the crown,
  Would with the scepter straight be strucken down?

"If Collatinus dream of my intent,
Will he not wake, and in a desp'rate rage
Post hither, this vile purpose to prevent?—   220
This siege that hath engirt his marriage,
This blur to youth, this sorrow to the sage,
  This dying virtue, this surviving shame,
  Whose crime will bear an ever-during blame.

"O what excuse can my invention make,   225
When thou shalt charge me with so black a deed?
Will not my tongue be mute, my frail joints shake,
Mine eyes forego their light, my false heart bleed?
The guilt being great, the fear doth still exceed;
  And extreme fear can neither fight nor fly,   230
  But coward-like with trembling terror die.

"Had Collatinus killed my son or sire,
Or lain in ambush to betray my life,
Or were he not my dear friend, this desire
Might have excuse to work upon his wife,   235
As in revenge or quittal of such strife;
  But as he is my kinsman, my dear friend,
  The shame and fault finds no excuse nor end.

"Shameful it is—ay, if the fact be known;
Hateful it is—there is no hate in loving;   240
I'll beg her love—but she is not her own;
The worst is but denial and reproving.

243. **My will . . . removing:** my lust is too strong to be curbed by weak reasoning.

244-45. **Who fears . . . in awe:** anyone who fears a moral commandment (*sentence*) or an old man's proverbial warning could be kept in check by the warning painted on hangings (*painted cloth*). Moralistic pictures painted on canvas were common in Shakespeare's age.

246. **graceless:** without divine help; **disputation:** debate.

247. **will:** lust.

248. **good thoughts . . . dispensation:** meaning, he twists his good thoughts to give him leave (*dispensation*) to commit evil.

259. **lawn:** sheer white fabric; cambric.

265. **Narcissus:** in Greek mythology, a youth so in love with his own image, which he saw reflected in a pool, that he pined away and died.

267. **color:** pretense.

269. **Poor . . . abuses:** some poor wretches suffer remorse for minor faults.

My will is strong, past reason's weak removing.—
  Who fears a sentence or an old man's saw
  Shall by a painted cloth be kept in awe."   245

Thus graceless holds he disputation
'Tween frozen conscience and hot-burning will,
And with good thoughts makes dispensation,
Urging the worser sense for vantage still;
Which in a moment doth confound and kill   250
  All pure effects, and doth so far proceed
  That what is vile shows like a virtuous deed.

Quoth he, "She took me kindly by the hand,
And gazed for tidings in my eager eyes,
Fearing some hard news from the warlike band   255
Where her beloved Collatinus lies.
O how her fear did make her color rise!
  First red as roses that on lawn we lay,
  Then white as lawn, the roses took away.

"And how her hand, in my hand being locked,   260
Forced it to tremble with her loyal fear!
Which struck her sad, and then it faster rocked
Until her husband's welfare she did hear;
Whereat she smiled with so sweet a cheer
  That had Narcissus seen her as she stood   265
  Self-love had never drowned him in the flood.

"Why hunt I then for color or excuses?
All orators are dumb when beauty pleadeth;
Poor wretches have remorse in poor abuses;
Love thrives not in the heart that shadows dreadeth; 270

271. **Affection:** lust.

274. **avaunt:** away.

275. **Respect:** prudence.

277. **beseems:** suits; **sage:** wise man.

286. **cross:** assail.

287. **league:** alliance; **invasion:** enmity; meaning that Tarquin is torn between persuasion to resist temptation and desire to commit his deed. This argument is like the combat between the Good and Evil Angels for the Soul of Man in the morality plays, and in Marlowe's *Doctor Faustus*.

291-92. **That . . . incline:** the sense is that the eye which contemplates the husband, Collatine, is purer and will not condone the sin that Tarquin's lust is about to cause.

295. **heartens up:** incites; **servile powers:** lower instincts.

296. **jocund:** cheerful.

298. **pride:** sexual appetite.

Affection is my captain, and he leadeth;
  And when his gaudy banner is displayed,
  The coward fights and will not be dismayed.

"Then childish fear avaunt! debating die!
Respect and reason wait on wrinkled age!   275
My heart shall never countermand mine eye;
Sad pause and deep regard beseems the sage;
My part is youth, and beats these from the stage:
  Desire my pilot is, beauty my prize;
  Then who fears sinking where such treasure lies?"   280

As corn o'ergrown by weeds, so heedful fear
Is almost choked by unresisted lust.
Away he steals with open list'ning ear,
Full of foul hope and full of fond mistrust;
Both which, as servitors to the unjust,   285
  So cross him with their opposite persuasion
  That now he vows a league, and now invasion.

Within his thought her heavenly image sits,
And in the selfsame seat sits Collatine.
That eye which looks on her confounds his wits;   290
That eye which him beholds, as more divine,
Unto a view so false will not incline;
  But with a pure appeal seeks to the heart,
  Which once corrupted takes the worser part;

And therein heartens up his servile powers,   295
Who, flattered by their leader's jocund show,
Stuff up his lust, as minutes fill up hours;
And as their captain, so their pride doth grow,

303. **retires his ward:** a technical expression describing the inner working of a lock.

304. **rate his ill:** a metaphor in which the poet imagines the noise of the lock serving as a rebuke to Tarquin.

305. **regard:** concern.

306. **threshold . . . heard:** another metaphor indicating that the door by its creaking wants to warn Lucrece.

318. **rushes:** rushes were used in Elizabethan times to cover the floor.

321. **inured:** used to.

324. **consters:** construes.

326. **accidental things of trial:** things put accidentally in his way.

Paying more slavish tribute than they owe.
  By reprobate desire thus madly led,   300
  The Roman lord marcheth to Lucrece' bed.

The locks between her chamber and his will,
Each one by him enforced, retires his ward;
But, as they open, they all rate his ill,
Which drives the creeping thief to some regard.   305
The threshold grates the door to have him heard;
  Night-wand'ring weasels shriek to see him there;
  They fright him, yet he still pursues his fear.

As each unwilling portal yields him way,
Through little vents and crannies of the place   310
The wind wars with his torch to make him stay,
And blows the smoke of it into his face,
Extinguishing his conduct in this case;
  But his hot heart, which fond desire doth scorch,
  Puffs forth another wind that fires the torch;   315

And being lighted, by the light he spies
Lucretia's glove, wherein her needle sticks;
He takes it from the rushes where it lies,
And griping it, the needle his finger pricks,
As who should say "This glove to wanton tricks   320
  Is not inured. Return again in haste;
  Thou see'st our mistress' ornaments are chaste."

But all these poor forbiddings could not stay him;
He in the worst sense consters their denial:
The doors, the wind, the glove, that did delay him,   325
He takes for accidental things of trial;

327. **bars:** lines on the face of watch or clock; **dial:** timepiece.

328. **let:** check.

330. **lets:** hindrances.

332. **prime:** spring of the year.

333. **sneaped:** nipped.

335. **shelves:** sandbanks.

341. **So . . . wrought:** impiety has so changed him from his better self.

342. **for his prey to pray:** this type of word play was popular with the Elizabethans; Tarquin is so carried away by impiety that he prays that his victim will be delivered to him.

346. **compass his fair fair:** persuade his virtuous beauty (Lucrece) to submit.

347. **they:** the eternal powers, represented as singular in line 345; he prays that the eternal powers will help him (*stand auspicious*) at this time.

348. **must deflower:** must rape.

349. **fact:** deed.

"Then Love and Fortune be my gods, my guide!"
Fortune astride the wheel so often associated with her.
From Vincenzo Cartari, *Imagines deorum* (1581).

Or as those bars which stop the hourly dial,
  Who with a ling'ring stay his course doth let,
  Till every minute pays the hour his debt.

"So, so," quoth he, "these lets attend the time,   330
Like little frosts that sometime threat the spring,
To add a more rejoicing to the prime,
And give the sneaped birds more cause to sing.
Pain pays the income of each precious thing;
  Huge rocks, high winds, strong pirates, shelves 335
    and sands
  The merchant fears, ere rich at home he lands."

Now is he come unto the chamber door
That shuts him from the heaven of his thought,
Which with a yielding latch, and with no more,
Hath barred him from the blessed thing he sought.   340
So from himself impiety hath wrought,
  That for his prey to pray he doth begin,
  As if the heavens should countenance his sin.

But in the midst of his unfruitful prayer,
Having solicited th'eternal power   345
That his foul thoughts might compass his fair fair,
And they would stand auspicious to the hour,
Even there he starts; quoth he "I must deflower:
  The powers to whom I pray abhor this fact;
  How can they then assist me in the act?   350

"Then Love and Fortune be my gods, my guide!
My will is backed with resolution.
Thoughts are but dreams till their effects be tried;

354. **absolution:** remission of sins through penance; Shakespeare is oblivious to the anachronism of making Tarquin use a term from Christian theology.

355. **love's . . . dissolution:** love's fire can dissolve the frost of fear.

356. **The eye of heaven is out:** the sun has set.

364. **mortal sting:** deadly lust, with a phallic metaphor implied.

366. **unstained:** uncontaminated.

367. **curtains being close:** the curtains around the bed being shut.

371. **cloud:** bed curtains; **silver moon:** Lucrece, here equated with Diana, the chaste moon goddess.

373. **bereaves:** robs.

375. **wink:** shut.

380. **period of their ill:** end of their wickedness.

Night owls with their prey. From Olaus Magnus, *Historia de gentibus* (1555).

The blackest sin is cleared with absolution;
Against love's fire fear's frost hath dissolution.   355
  The eye of heaven is out, and misty night
  Covers the shame that follows sweet delight."

This said, his guilty hand plucked up the latch,
And with his knee the door he opens wide.
The dove sleeps fast that this night-owl will catch.   360
Thus treason works ere traitors be espied.
Who sees the lurking serpent steps aside;
  But she, sound sleeping, fearing no such thing,
  Lies at the mercy of his mortal sting.

Into the chamber wickedly he stalks   365
And gazeth on her yet unstained bed.
The curtains being close, about he walks,
Rolling his greedy eyeballs in his head.
By their high treason is his heart misled,
  Which gives the watchword to his hand full soon   370
  To draw the cloud that hides the silver moon.

Look as the fair and fiery-pointed sun,
Rushing from forth a cloud, bereaves our sight;
Even so, the curtain drawn, his eyes begun
To wink, being blinded with a greater light;   375
Whether it is that she reflects so bright
  That dazzleth them, or else some shame supposed,
  But blind they are, and keep themselves enclosed.

O, had they in that darksome prison died!
Then had they seen the period of their ill;   380
Then Collatine again, by Lucrece' side,

382. **clear:** uncontaminated.

383. **blessed league:** holy marriage (between Lucrece and Collatine).

385. **sell:** give up.

387. **Coz'ning:** cheating.

389. **to want his bliss:** because it lacks its happiness, the pillow puffs out on each side, a somewhat strained metaphor.

392. **unhallowed:** unholy.

393. **Without the bed:** outside the bedcovers.

401. **wantons:** unruly hair.

405. **twain:** both.

The lion with his prey. From Arnold Freitag, *Mythologia ethica* (1579).

In his clear bed might have reposed still;
But they must ope, this blessed league to kill;
  And holy-thoughted Lucrece to their sight
    Must sell her joy, her life, her world's delight.   385

Her lily hand her rosy cheek lies under,
Coz'ning the pillow of a lawful kiss;
Who, therefore angry, seems to part in sunder,
Swelling on either side to want his bliss;
Between whose hills her head entombed is;   390
  Where, like a virtuous monument, she lies,
    To be admired of lewd unhallowed eyes.

Without the bed her other fair hand was,
On the green coverlet; whose perfect white
Showed like an April daisy on the grass,   395
With pearly sweat resembling dew of night.
Her eyes, like marigolds, had sheathed their light,
  And canopied in darkness sweetly lay,
    Till they might open to adorn the day.

Her hair, like golden threads, played with her 400
  breath—
O modest wantons! wanton modesty!—
Showing life's triumph in the map of death,
And death's dim look in life's mortality:
Each in her sleep themselves so beautify
  As if between them twain there were no strife,   405
    But that life lived in death and death in life.

Her breasts, like ivory globes circled with blue,
A pair of maiden worlds unconquered,

409. **bearing yoke:** oppressive touch.

411. **ambition:** lust.

413. **heave the owner out:** usurp the rights of the husband.

417. **will . . . tired:** will here as elsewhere in the poem is synonymous with lust; Tarquin satiates himself with his lustful gaze.

419. **alablaster:** alabaster.

421. **fawneth:** delights in.

422. **Sharp hunger . . . satisfied:** the satisfaction of conquest relieves the sharp pangs of appetite.

424. **qualified:** modified; eased.

425. **Slacked, not suppressed:** eased but not ended.

427. **uproar:** surging desire.

428. **pillage:** loot.

429. **Obdurate vassals:** stubborn henchmen; **fell exploits:** evil deeds.

432. **Swell:** grow violent.

433. **alarum:** alarm.

436. **His eye . . . hand:** the vision of Lucrece leads Tarquin to want to touch her.

Save of their lord no bearing yoke they knew,
And him by oath they truly honored.   410
These worlds in Tarquin new ambition bred,
  Who like a foul usurper went about
  From this fair throne to heave the owner out.

What could he see but mightily he noted?
What did he note but strongly he desired?   415
What he beheld, on that he firmly doted,
And in his will his willful eye he tired.
With more than admiration he admired
  Her azure veins, her alablaster skin,
  Her coral lips, her snow-white dimpled chin.   420

As the grim lion fawneth o'er his prey,
Sharp hunger by the conquest satisfied,
So o'er this sleeping soul doth Tarquin stay,
His rage of lust by gazing qualified;
Slacked, not suppressed; for standing by her side,   425
  His eye, which late this mutiny restrains,
  Unto a greater uproar tempts his veins;

And they, like straggling slaves for pillage fighting,
Obdurate vassals fell exploits effecting,
In bloody death and ravishment delighting,   430
Nor children's tears nor mothers' groans respecting,
Swell in their pride, the onset still expecting.
  Anon his beating heart, alarum striking,
  Gives the hot charge, and bids them do their liking.

His drumming heart cheers up his burning eye,   435
His eye commends the leading to his hand;

438. **Smoking with pride:** steaming with desire.

442. **cabinet:** heart, mistress of the blood in the veins; the metaphor is strained, but the sense is that Lucrece's consciousness lies within the heart (*the quiet cabinet*) which presently warns her of danger.

448. **dimmed and controlled:** dazzled and subdued.

450. **fancy:** fantasy; nightmare.

451. **ghastly sprite:** ghostly spirit.

452. **aspect:** appearance.

453. **worser taking:** in worse plight.

458-59. **yet, winking . . . antics:** closing her eyes to avoid an unpleasant sight, she sees fantastic figures (*antics*).

460. **forgeries:** imaginings.

A battering ram, used by Roman legions to break down a wall. From Guillaume Du Choul, *Discours de la religion des anciens Romains* (1581).

His hand, as proud of such a dignity,
Smoking with pride, marched on to make his stand
On her bare breast, the heart of all her land;
  Whose ranks of blue veins as his hand did scale,   440
  Left their round turrets destitute and pale.

They, must'ring to the quiet cabinet
Where their dear governess and lady lies,
Do tell her she is dreadfully beset,
And fright her with confusion of their cries.   445
She, much amazed, breaks ope her locked-up eyes,
  Who, peeping forth this tumult to behold,
  Are by his flaming torch dimmed and controlled.

Imagine her as one in dead of night
From forth dull sleep by dreadful fancy waking,   450
That thinks she hath beheld some ghastly sprite,
Whose grim aspect sets every joint a-shaking;
What terror 'tis! but she, in worser taking,
  From sleep disturbed, heedfully doth view
  The sight which makes supposed terror true.   455

Wrapped and confounded in a thousand fears,
Like to a new-killed bird she trembling lies;
She dares not look; yet, winking, there appears
Quick-shifting antics, ugly in her eyes.
Such shadows are the weak brain's forgeries,   460
  Who, angry that the eyes fly from their lights,
  In darkness daunts them with more dreadful sights.

His hand that yet remains upon her breast—
Rude ram, to batter such an ivory wall!—

467. **bulk:** body.

471. **heartless:** disheartened; frightened.

474. **by dumb demeanor:** by making signs.

475. **urgeth:** demands to know.

483. **For those . . . mine:** for the beauty in your eyes makes it impossible for me not to desire you.

484. **forestall:** prevent.

491. **crosses:** troubles.

"First like a trumpet doth his tongue begin
To sound a parley to his heartless foe."
Roman trumpeters. From Du Choul, *Discours* (1581).

May feel her heart, poor citizen, distressed,   465
Wounding itself to death, rise up and fall,
Beating her bulk, that his hand shakes withal.
 This moves in him more rage and lesser pity,
 To make the breach and enter this sweet city.

First like a trumpet doth his tongue begin   470
To sound a parley to his heartless foe,
Who o'er the white sheet peers her whiter chin,
The reason of this rash alarm to know,
Which he by dumb demeanor seeks to show;
 But she with vehement prayers urgeth still   475
 Under what color he commits this ill.

Thus he replies: "The color in thy face,
That even for anger makes the lily pale
And the red rose blush at her own disgrace,
Shall plead for me and tell my loving tale.   480
Under that color am I come to scale
 Thy never-conquered fort. The fault is thine,
 For those thine eyes betray thee unto mine.

"Thus I forestall thee, if thou mean to chide:
Thy beauty hath ensnared thee to this night,   485
Where thou with patience must my will abide,
My will that marks thee for my earth's delight,
Which I to conquer sought with all my might;
 But as reproof and reason beat it dead,
 By thy bright beauty was it newly bred.   490

"I see what crosses my attempt will bring;
I know what thorns the growing rose defends;

494. **beforehand counsel:** advice that his conscience had previously given him.

495. **heedful friends:** friends concerned about him.

502. **ensue the deed:** will follow the crime.

504. **Yet . . . infamy:** and still I rush headlong to my disgrace.

505. **blade:** sword.

507. **Coucheth the fowl:** causes the bird to hug the ground.

509. **insulting falchion:** gloating sword.

510. **marking:** listening to.

520. **every open eye:** everyone who sees.

". . . he shakes aloft his Roman blade,
Which, like a falcon tow'ring in the skies,
Coucheth the fowl below with his wings' shade"
From Francis Barlow, *Various Birds and Beasts* (ca. 1755).

I think the honey guarded with a sting;
All this beforehand counsel comprehends.
But will is deaf and hears no heedful friends;   495
   Only he hath an eye to gaze on beauty,
   And dotes on what he looks, 'gainst law or duty.

"I have debated, even in my soul,
What wrong, what shame, what sorrow I shall breed;
But nothing can affection's course control,   500
Or stop the headlong fury of his speed.
I know repentant tears ensue the deed,
   Reproach, disdain and deadly enmity;
   Yet strive I to embrace mine infamy."

This said, he shakes aloft his Roman blade,   505
Which, like a falcon tow'ring in the skies,
Coucheth the fowl below with his wings' shade,
Whose crooked beak threats if he mount he dies.
So under his insulting falchion lies
   Harmless Lucretia, marking what he tells   510
   With trembling fear, as fowl hear falcons' bells.

"Lucrece," quoth he, "this night I must enjoy thee.
If thou deny, then force must work my way,
For in thy bed I purpose to destroy thee;
That done, some worthless slave of thine I'll slay,   515
To kill thine honor with thy life's decay;
   And in thy dead arms do I mean to place him,
   Swearing I slew him, seeing thee embrace him.

"So thy surviving husband shall remain
The scornful mark of every open eye;   520

521. **disdain:** contemptible deed.

522. **blurred:** stained.

523. **obloquy:** shame.

524. **in rhymes:** in rhyming ballads, which often reported sensational crimes.

529. **For . . . enacted:** because the legal status will appear unchanged.

530. **simple:** herb; **compacted:** made into a medical prescription.

534. **Tender:** listen to; heed.

537. **slavish wipe:** a slave's brand mark.

538. **descried:** seen; **in men's nativity:** at men's birth.

540. **cockatrice:** mythological creature whose looks could kill.

543. **hind:** female deer; **gripe:** a griffin; another mythological creature, half lion and half eagle.

546. **Nor aught:** nothing.

The cockatrice, or basilisk, a legendary beast reputed to be half cock, half reptile, whose glance was fatal. From Freitag, *Mythologia* (1579).

Thy kinsmen hang their heads at this disdain,
Thy issue blurred with nameless bastardy;
And thou, the author of their obloquy,
Shalt have thy trespass cited up in rhymes
And sung by children in succeeding times.   525

"But if thou yield, I rest thy secret friend:
The fault unknown is as a thought unacted;
A little harm done to a great good end
For lawful policy remains enacted.
The poisonous simple sometime is compacted   530
In a pure compound; being so applied,
His venom in effect is purified.

"Then, for thy husband and thy children's sake,
Tender my suit; bequeath not to their lot
The shame that from them no device can take,   535
The blemish that will never be forgot;
Worse than a slavish wipe or birth-hour's blot;
For marks descried in men's nativity
Are nature's faults, not their own infamy."

Here with a cockatrice' dead-killing eye   540
He rouseth up himself, and makes a pause;
While she, the picture of pure piety,
Like a white hind under the gripe's sharp claws,
Pleads in a wilderness where are no laws
To the rough beast that knows no gentle right,   545
Nor aught obeys but his foul appetite.

But when a black-faced cloud the world doth threat,
In his dim mist th'aspiring mountains hiding,

550. **biding:** abiding place.

552. **delays:** delay; the subject of the verb is *words*.

553. **And moody . . . plays:** Pluto, god of the Underworld, pleased and drowsy with music played by Orpheus, allowed Orpheus' wife, Eurydice, to return from Hades on condition that Orpheus would not look back, a condition that he did not keep.

554. **night-waking:** being awake in the night.

555. **hold-fast foot:** claw that grasps tightly.

557. **A swallowing . . . wanteth:** an enveloping sea of lust unsatisfied even by the plenty of Lucrece's beauty.

559. **plaining:** pleading.

562. **remorseless wrinkles:** unpitying frowns.

565. **She puts . . . place:** she talks in broken sentences, with full stops in the wrong places.

568. **conjures:** entreats.

571. **common troth:** ordinary fidelity.

573. **borrowed bed:** bed which he occupies as a guest.

574. **stoop:** yield.

From earth's dark womb some gentle gust doth get,
Which blows these pitchy vapors from their biding,   550
Hind'ring their present fall by this dividing;
    So his unhallowed haste her words delays,
    And moody Pluto winks while Orpheus plays.

Yet, foul night-waking cat, he doth but dally,
While in his hold-fast foot the weak mouse panteth;   555
Her sad behavior feeds his vulture folly,
A swallowing gulf that even in plenty wanteth;
His ear her prayers admits, but his heart granteth
    No penetrable entrance to her plaining.
    Tears harden lust, though marble wear with   560
      raining.

Her pity-pleading eyes are sadly fixed
In the remorseless wrinkles of his face;
Her modest eloquence with sighs is mixed,
Which to her oratory adds more grace.
She puts the period often from his place,   565
    And midst the sentence so her accent breaks
    That twice she doth begin ere once she speaks.

She conjures him by high almighty Jove,
By knighthood, gentry, and sweet friendship's oath,
By her untimely tears, her husband's love,   570
By holy human law and common troth,
By heaven and earth, and all the power of both,
    That to his borrowed bed he make retire,
    And stoop to honor, not to foul desire.

Quoth she: "Reward not hospitality   575

579. **shoot:** shot.

580. **woodman:** hunter.

585. **Thou look'st not like deceit:** you do not look like a betrayer.

586. **heave thee:** throw you out.

590. **wrack-threat'ning:** ruin-threatening.

592. **convert:** alter.

596. **In Tarquin's likeness:** Lucrece implies that the ravisher cannot be Tarquin but must be someone masquerading in his likeness.

603-604. **How will . . . spring:** how great will thy shame mature (*be seeded*) when you come of age when in your youth your vices thus begin.

With such black payment as thou hast pretended;
Mud not the fountain that gave drink to thee;
Mar not the thing that cannot be amended;
End thy ill aim before thy shoot be ended.
   He is no woodman that doth bend his bow   580
   To strike a poor unseasonable doe.

"My husband is thy friend—for his sake spare me;
Thyself art mighty—for thine own sake leave me;
Myself a weakling—do not then ensnare me;
Thou look'st not like deceit—do not deceive me.   585
My sighs like whirlwinds labor hence to heave thee.
   If ever man were moved with woman's moans,
   Be moved with my tears, my sighs, my groans;

"All which together, like a troubled ocean,
Beat at thy rocky and wrack-threat'ning heart,   590
To soften it with their continual motion;
For stones dissolved to water do convert.
O, if no harder than a stone thou art,
   Melt at my tears, and be compassionate!
   Soft pity enters at an iron gate.   595

"In Tarquin's likeness I did entertain thee;
Hast thou put on his shape to do him shame?
To all the host of heaven I complain me
Thou wrong'st his honor, wound'st his princely name.
Thou art not what thou seem'st; and if the same,   600
   Thou seem'st not what thou art, a god, a king;
   For kings like gods should govern every thing.

"How will thy shame be seeded in thine age,

605. **in thy hope:** while still aspiring to the throne.

607. **be remembered:** let it be remembered.

608-609. **From vassal . . . clay:** the meaning is that if the misdeeds of a subject cannot be expunged, certainly the crimes of a king cannot be hidden.

612. **perforce:** of necessity.

615. **glass:** mirror.

622. **back'st:** uphold; **laud:** praise.

623. **bawd:** obscene character.

When thus thy vices bud before thy spring?
If in thy hope thou dar'st do such outrage,   605
What dar'st thou not when once thou art a king?
O, be remembered, no outrageous thing
   From vassal actors can be wiped away;
   Then kings' misdeeds cannot be hid in clay.

"This deed will make thee only loved for fear,   610
But happy monarchs still are feared for love;
With foul offenders thou perforce must bear,
When they in thee the like offences prove.
If but for fear of this, thy will remove;
   For princes are the glass, the school, the book,   615
   Where subjects' eyes do learn, do read, do look.

"And wilt thou be the school where Lust shall learn?
Must he in thee read lectures of such shame?
Wilt thou be glass wherein it shall discern
Authority for sin, warrant for blame,   620
To privilege dishonor in thy name?
   Thou back'st reproach against long-living laud,
   And mak'st fair reputation but a bawd.

"Hast thou command? By him that gave it thee,
From a pure heart command thy rebel will;   625
Draw not thy sword to guard iniquity,
For it was lent thee all that brood to kill.
Thy princely office how canst thou fulfill,
   When patterned by thy fault foul sin may say
   He learned to sin, and thou didst teach the way?   630

632. **trespass:** sin.

637. **askance:** turn aside; that is, men wrapped in their iniquity, turn their eyes from their own misdeeds.

638. **heaved-up:** upraised.

639. **lust, thy rash relier:** lust, on which you rashly rely.

640. **I sue . . . repeal:** I beg for a return of the true prince from exile; Lucrece's fancy is that her seducer is not Tarquin in his true incarnation.

641. **flatt'ring:** caressing.

643. **doting eyne:** besotted eyes.

650-51. **salt sovereign . . . taste:** salt sovereign is the sea. The metaphor means that the streams of fresh water rushing to the sea may swell the volume but will not alter the salt taste.

657. **puddle's womb is hearsed:** puddle means muddy water; his sea will be confined to a pool of muddy water as in a narrow coffin.

"Think but how vile a spectacle it were
To view thy present trespass in another.
Men's faults do seldom to themselves appear;
Their own transgressions partially they smother;
This guilt would seem death-worthy in thy brother.   635
  O, how are they wrapped in with infamies
  That from their own misdeeds askance their eyes!

"To thee, to thee, my heaved-up hands appeal,
Not to seducing lust, thy rash relier;
I sue for exiled majesty's repeal;   640
Let him return, and flatt'ring thoughts retire.
His true respect will prison false desire,
  And wipe the dim mist from thy doting eyne,
  That thou shalt see thy state and pity mine."

"Have done," quoth he, "my uncontrolled tide   645
Turns not, but swells the higher by this let.
Small lights are soon blown out, huge fires abide,
And with the wind in greater fury fret.
The petty streams that pay a daily debt
  To their salt sovereign, with their fresh falls' haste   650
  Add to his flow, but alter not his taste."

"Thou art," quoth she, "a sea, a sovereign king;
And, lo, there falls into thy boundless flood
Black lust, dishonor, shame, misgoverning,
Who seek to stain the ocean of thy blood.   655
If all these petty ills shall change thy good,
  Thy sea within a puddle's womb is hearsed,
  And not the puddle in thy sea dispersed.

666. **low vassals:** slaves.

669. **coy:** caressing.

678. **white fleece:** night clothes; **controlled:** stopped.

"The wolf hath seized his prey, the poor lamb cries" From Freitag, *Mythologia* (1579).

"So shall these slaves be king, and thou their slave;
Thou nobly base, they basely dignified;   660
Thou their fair life, and they thy fouler grave;
Thou loathed in their shame, they in thy pride.
The lesser thing should not the greater hide;
  The cedar stoops not to the base shrub's foot,
  But low shrubs wither at the cedar's root.   665

"So let thy thoughts, low vassals to thy state"—
"No more," quoth he; "by heaven, I will not hear thee.
Yield to my love; if not, enforced hate,
Instead of love's coy touch, shall rudely tear thee;
That done, despitefully I mean to bear thee   670
  Unto the base bed of some rascal groom,
  To be thy partner in this shameful doom."

This said, he sets his foot upon the light,
For light and lust are deadly enemies;
Shame folded up in blind concealing night,   675
When most unseen, then most doth tyrannize.
The wolf hath seized his prey, the poor lamb cries,
  Till with her own white fleece her voice controlled
  Entombs her outcry in her lips' sweet fold;

For with the nightly linen that she wears   680
He pens her piteous clamors in her head,
Cooling his hot face in the chastest tears
That ever modest eyes with sorrow shed.
O, that prone lust should stain so pure a bed!
  The spots whereof could weeping purify,   685
  Her tears should drop on them perpetually.

689. **league:** union.
695. **Unapt:** unfit; **tender smell:** faint scent.
696. **balk:** miss; leave untouched.
701. **conceit:** conception; notion; understanding.
702. **still:** quiet.
703. **receipt:** that which has been received.
707. **jade:** worn-out horse.
710. **recreant:** craven; faithless.
711. **bankrout:** bankrupt.
714. **remission:** remission of sins; forgiveness.

But she hath lost a dearer thing than life,
And he hath won what he would lose again.
This forced league doth force a further strife;
This momentary joy breeds months of pain;   690
This hot desire converts to cold disdain;
    Pure Chastity is rifled of her store,
    And Lust, the thief, far poorer than before.

Look as the full-fed hound or gorged hawk,
Unapt for tender smell or speedy flight,   695
Make slow pursuit, or altogether balk
The prey wherein by nature they delight,
So surfeit-taking Tarquin fares this night:
    His taste delicious, in digestion souring,
    Devours his will, that lived by foul devouring.   700

O, deeper sin than bottomless conceit
Can comprehend in still imagination!
Drunken Desire must vomit his receipt,
Ere he can see his own abomination.
While Lust is in his pride, no exclamation   705
    Can curb his heat or rein his rash desire,
    Till, like a jade, Self-will himself doth tire.

And then with lank and lean discolored cheek,
With heavy eye, knit brow, and strengthless pace,
Feeble Desire, all recreant, poor and meek,   710
Like to a bankrout beggar wails his case:
The flesh being proud, Desire doth fight with Grace,
    For there it revels, and when that decays
    The guilty rebel for remission prays.

721. **spotted princess:** Tarquin's soul.

722. **She:** his soul; **subjects:** emotions.

724. **mortal:** deadly.

725. **thrall:** slave.

727. **prescience:** foreknowledge.

733. **spoil:** injured one (Lucrece).

740. **faintly:** faint-heartedly.

741. **direful:** terrible.

"She says her subjects with foul insurrection
Have battered down her consecrated wall"
An emblem depicting "intestine strife," or civil war. From
Whitney's *A Choice of Emblems* (1586).

So fares it with this faultful lord of Rome,   715
Who this accomplishment so hotly chased;
For now against himself he sounds this doom,
That through the length of times he stands disgraced;
Besides, his soul's fair temple is defaced,
  To whose weak ruins muster troops of cares,   720
  To ask the spotted princess how she fares.

She says her subjects with foul insurrection
Have battered down her consecrated wall,
And by their mortal fault brought in subjection
Her immortality, and made her thrall   725
To living death and pain perpetual;
  Which in her prescience she controlled still,
  But her foresight could not forestall their will.

Ev'n in this thought through the dark night he
    stealeth,
A captive victor that hath lost in gain;   730
Bearing away the wound that nothing healeth,
The scar that will, despite of cure, remain;
Leaving his spoil perplexed in greater pain.
  She bears the load of lust he left behind,
  And he the burden of a guilty mind.   735

He like a thievish dog creeps sadly thence;
She like a wearied lamb lies panting there;
He scowls, and hates himself for his offence;
She, desperate, with her nails her flesh doth tear;
He faintly flies, sweating with guilty fear;   740
  She stays, exclaiming on the direful night;
  He runs, and chides his vanished, loathed delight.

743. **heavy convertite:** gloomy convert.

747. **scapes:** escapades; deeds; **open lay:** reveal.

749. **To cloak:** to hide.

755. **grave:** engrave; **water:** aqua fortis (nitric acid), used in engraving.

762. **spite:** vexation.

763. **Against:** upon.

765. **notary:** recorder.

766. **fell:** evil.

768. **defame:** defamation.

He thence departs a heavy convertite;
She there remains a hopeless castaway;
He in his speed looks for the morning light;　　　745
She prays she never may behold the day.
"For day," quoth she, "night's scapes doth open lay,
　　And my true eyes have never practiced how
　　To cloak offences with a cunning brow.

"They think not but that every eye can see　　　750
The same disgrace which they themselves behold;
And therefore would they still in darkness be,
To have their unseen sin remain untold;
For they their guilt with weeping will unfold,
　　And grave, like water that doth eat in steel,　　　755
　　Upon my cheeks what helpless shame I feel."

Here she exclaims against repose and rest,
And bids her eyes hereafter still be blind.
She wakes her heart by beating on her breast,
And bids it leap from thence, where it may find　　　760
Some purer chest to close so pure a mind.
　　Frantic with grief thus breathes she forth her spite
　　Against the unseen secrecy of night:

"O comfort-killing Night, image of hell!
Dim register and notary of shame!　　　765
Black stage for tragedies and murders fell!
Vast sin-concealing chaos! nurse of blame!
Blind muffled bawd! dark harbor for defame!
　　Grim cave of death! whisp'ring conspirator
　　With close-tongued treason and the ravisher!　　　770

773. **eastern light:** dawn.

774. **proportioned:** regulated.

776. **wonted:** usual.

780. **supreme fair:** sun god.

781. **arrive:** reach; **noontide prick:** noon marking on the sundial.

786. **silver-shining queen:** the moon-goddess; the moon.

787. **twinkling handmaids:** the stars.

790. **And fellowship . . . assuage:** proverbial; cf., "Misery loves company."

791. **palmers':** pilgrims'.

796. **silver brine:** tears.

"The silver-shining queen": Diana, the moon-goddess. From Vincenzo Cartari, *Imagini de gli dei delli antichi* (1615).

O hateful, vaporous and foggy Night!
Since thou art guilty of my cureless crime,
Muster thy mists to meet the eastern light,
Make war against proportioned course of time;
Or if thou wilt permit the sun to climb   775
    His wonted height, yet ere he go to bed,
    Knit poisonous clouds about his golden head.

"With rotten damps ravish the morning air;
Let their exhaled unwholesome breaths make sick
The life of purity, the supreme fair,   780
Ere he arrive his weary noontide prick;
And let thy musty vapors march so thick
    That in their smoky ranks his smothered light
    May set at noon and make perpetual night.

"Were Tarquin Night, as he is but Night's child,   785
The silver-shining queen he would distain;
Her twinkling handmaids too, by him defiled,
Through Night's black bosom should not peep again;
So should I have copartners in my pain;
    And fellowship in woe doth woe assuage,   790
    As palmers' chat makes short their pilgrimage.

"Where now I have no one to blush with me,
To cross their arms and hang their heads with mine,
To mask their brows and hide their infamy;
But I alone alone must sit and pine,   795
Seasoning the earth with show'rs of silver brine,
    Mingling my talk with tears, my grief with groans,
    Poor wasting monuments of lasting moans.

805. **sepulchered:** entombed.

806. **Make me . . . Day:** make me not an object of scorn to the telltale day.

807. **charactered:** written.

811. **cipher:** interpret.

817. **Feast-finding minstrels:** banquet-haunting minstrels.

818. **tie:** hold the attention of; **attend:** hear.

820. **senseless reputation:** reputation untarnished with sensuality.

822. **disputation:** argument; debate.

825. **attaint:** stain.

"O Night, thou furnace of foul-reeking smoke,
Let not the jealous Day behold that face   800
Which underneath thy black all-hiding cloak
Immodestly lies martyred with disgrace!
Keep still possession of thy gloomy place,
  That all the faults which in thy reign are made
  May likewise be sepulchered in thy shade!   805

"Make me not object to the telltale Day.
The light will show, charactered in my brow,
The story of sweet chastity's decay,
The impious breach of holy wedlock vow;
Yea, the illiterate, that know not how   810
  To cipher what is writ in learned books,
  Will quote my loathsome trespass in my looks.

"The nurse, to still her child, will tell my story,
And fright her crying babe with Tarquin's name;
The orator, to deck his oratory,   815
Will couple my reproach to Tarquin's shame;
Feast-finding minstrels, tuning my defame,
  Will tie the hearers to attend each line,
  How Tarquin wronged me, I Collatine.

"Let my good name, that senseless reputation,   820
For Collatine's dear love be kept unspotted;
If that be made a theme for disputation,
The branches of another root are rotted,
And undeserved reproach to him allotted
  That is as clear from this attaint of mine   825
  As I ere this was pure to Collatine.

828. **crest-wounding:** injury that damages one's personal honor; crest is derived from heraldry.

830. **mot:** motto, as on a coat-of-arms.

850. **founts:** springs.

852. **behests:** laws.

Toads in "venom mud." From *Hortus sanitatis* (1536).

"O unseen shame! invisible disgrace!
O unfelt sore! crest-wounding, private scar!
Reproach is stamped in Collatinus' face,
And Tarquin's eye may read the mot afar,   830
How he in peace is wounded, not in war.
  Alas, how many bear such shameful blows,
   Which not themselves, but he that gives them
    knows!

"If, Collatine, thine honor lay in me,
From me by strong assault it is bereft.   835
My honey lost, and I, a drone-like bee,
Have no perfection of my summer left,
But robbed and ransacked by injurious theft.
  In thy weak hive a wand'ring wasp hath crept,
  And sucked the honey which thy chaste bee kept.   840

"Yet am I guilty of thy honor's wrack;
Yet for thy honor did I entertain him;
Coming from thee, I could not put him back,
For it had been dishonor to disdain him;
Besides, of weariness he did complain him,   845
  And talked of virtue: O unlooked-for evil,
  When virtue is profaned in such a devil!

"Why should the worm intrude the maiden bud?
Or hateful cuckoos hatch in sparrows' nests?
Or toads infect fair founts with venom mud?   850
Or tyrant folly lurk in gentle breasts?
Or kings be breakers of their own behests?
  But no perfection is so absolute
  That some impurity doth not pollute.

855. **coffers up:** hoards in a chest.

858. **still-pining Tantalus:** Homer in the *Odyssey* (XI, 590 ff.) describes Tantalus as ever-hungry, standing in water neck deep, with fruits just above his reach. When he opens his mouth to drink or eat, the water and the fruit recede out of his reach. From this legend comes our word *tantalize.*

859. **barns:** stores.

863. **mastered:** possessed.

869. **Unruly blasts:** icy winds.

874. **ill-annexed Opportunity:** evil-connected occasion.

875. **Or kills:** either kills.

879. **point'st the season:** appoints the time.

880. **spurn'st at:** shows disdain for.

Opportunity, grasped by the forelock. The Roman officer in this sixteenth-century emblem would have reminded many readers of Tarquin, whose story was well known. From Jean Jacques Boissard, *Emblematum liber* (1588).

"The aged man that coffers up his gold   855
Is plagued with cramps and gouts and painful fits,
And scarce hath eyes his treasure to behold,
But like still-pining Tantalus he sits,
And useless barns the harvest of his wits,
  Having no other pleasure of his gain   860
  But torment that it cannot cure his pain.

"So then he hath it when he cannot use it,
And leaves it to be mastered by his young;
Who in their pride do presently abuse it.
Their father was too weak, and they too strong,   865
To hold their cursed-blessed fortune long.
  The sweets we wish for turn to loathed sours
  Even in the moment that we call them ours.

"Unruly blasts wait on the tender spring;
Unwholesome weeds take root with precious flowers: 870
The adder hisses where the sweet birds sing;
What virtue breeds iniquity devours.
We have no good that we can say is ours
  But ill-annexed Opportunity
  Or kills his life or else his quality.   875

"O Opportunity, thy guilt is great!
'Tis thou that execut'st the traitor's treason;
Thou sets the wolf where he the lamb may get;
Whoever plots the sin, thou point'st the season;
'Tis thou that spurn'st at right, at law, at reason; 880
  And in thy shady cell, where none may spy him,
  Sits Sin, to seize the souls that wander by him.

883. **vestal:** vestal virgin.
884. **temperance is thawed:** chastity is tempted.
892. **smoothing:** flattering; **ragged:** contemptible.
897. **suppliant's:** petitioner's.
898. **suit:** entreaty; something begged for.
899. **sort:** find.
901. **physic:** medicine.
902. **creep:** cripple.
905. **pines:** perishes.
910. **heinous:** atrocious.

Vestal virgins, consecrated to Vesta, were responsible for keeping the sacred fire alight. They were subject to burial alive if they broke their oath of chastity. From Cartari, *Imagini* (1609).

"Thou mak'st the vestal violate her oath;
Thou blow'st the fire when temperance is thawed;
Thou smother'st honesty, thou murd'rest troth;   885
Thou foul abettor! thou notorious bawd!
Thou plantest scandal and displacest laud.
  Thou ravisher, thou traitor, thou false thief,
  Thy honey turns to gall, thy joy to grief!

"Thy secret pleasure turns to open shame,   890
Thy private feasting to a public fast,
Thy smoothing titles to a ragged name,
Thy sugared tongue to bitter wormwood taste;
Thy violent vanities can never last.
  How comes it then, vile Opportunity,   895
  Being so bad, such numbers seek for thee?

"When wilt thou be the humble suppliant's friend,
And bring him where his suit may be obtained?
When wilt thou sort an hour great strifes to end?
Or free that soul which wretchedness hath chained?   900
Give physic to the sick, ease to the pained?
  The poor, lame, blind, halt, creep, cry out for thee;
  But they ne'er meet with Opportunity.

"The patient dies while the physician sleeps;
The orphan pines while the oppressor feeds;   905
Justice is feasting while the widow weeps;
Advice is sporting while infection breeds;
Thou grant'st no time for charitable deeds;
  Wrath, envy, treason, rape, and murder's rages,
  Thy heinous hours wait on them as their pages.   910

914. **gratis:** free; **appaid:** paid.

917. **stayed:** prevented.

919. **subornation:** in law, the act of procuring someone to bear false witness; commit perjury.

920. **shift:** fraud.

925. **copesmate:** bedfellow.

926. **post:** mail carrier; **grisly:** grim and ghastly.

928. **Base watch of woes:** servile watchman of sorrows.

936. **to fine:** to put an end to.

937. **opinion:** rumor.

938. **Not . . . bed:** destroy the reputation of a legal marriage.

Time, eater of youth. From Francis Petrarch, *Il Petrarca*, ed. Allessandro Vellutello (1560).

"When Truth and Virtue have to do with thee,
A thousand crosses keep them from thy aid;
They buy thy help, but Sin ne'er gives a fee;
He gratis comes, and thou art well appaid
As well to hear as grant what he hath said.   915
  My Collatine would else have come to me
  When Tarquin did, but he was stayed by thee.

"Guilty thou art of murder and of theft,
Guilty of perjury and subornation,
Guilty of treason, forgery and shift,   920
Guilty of incest, that abomination;
An accessory by thine inclination
  To all sins past and all that are to come,
  From the creation to the general doom.

"Misshapen Time, copesmate of ugly Night,   925
Swift subtle post, carrier of grisly care,
Eater of youth, false slave to false delight,
Base watch of woes, sin's pack-horse, virtue's snare;
Thou nursest all and murd'rest all that are.
  O, hear me then, injurious, shifting Time!   930
  Be guilty of my death, since of my crime.

"Why hath thy servant Opportunity
Betrayed the hours thou gavest me to repose,
Cancelled my fortunes and enchained me
To endless date of never-ending woes?   935
Time's office is to fine the hate of foes,
  To eat up errors by opinion bred,
  Not spend the dowry of a lawful bed.

942. sentinel the night: stand watch in the night.

943. wrong the wronger . . . right: punish the wrongdoer until he makes amends.

950. cherish springs: this phrase has puzzled critics. *Springs* may mean springs of water or possibly "shoots" or "sprigs." The word *cherish* has also puzzled editors; various meanings have been suggested including the emendation to "perish."

953. beldam: grandmother.

957. To mock . . . beguiled: to mock too-clever men who have fooled themselves with their own subtlety.

959. waste: wear down.

962. retiring: returning.

966. wrack: wreck.

"And turn the giddy round of Fortune's wheel"
From Gregar Reisch, *Margarita philosophica* (1517).

"Time's glory is to calm contending kings,
To unmask falsehood and bring truth to light,   940
To stamp the seal of time in aged things,
To wake the morn and sentinel the night,
To wrong the wronger till he render right,
  To ruinate proud buildings with thy hours
  And smear with dust their glitt'ring golden towers; 945

"To fill with wormholes stately monuments,
To feed oblivion with decay of things,
To blot old books and alter their contents,
To pluck the quills from ancient ravens' wings,
To dry the old oak's sap and cherish springs,   950
  To spoil antiquities of hammered steel
  And turn the giddy round of Fortune's wheel;

"To show the beldam daughters of her daughter,
To make the child a man, the man a child,
To slay the tiger that doth live by slaughter,   955
To tame the unicorn and lion wild,
To mock the subtle in themselves beguiled,
  To cheer the plowman with increaseful crops,
  And waste huge stones with little waterdrops.

"Why work'st thou mischief in thy pilgrimage,   960
Unless thou couldst return to make amends?
One poor retiring minute in an age
Would purchase thee a thousand thousand friends,
Lending him wit that to bad debtors lends.
  O, this dread night, wouldst thou one hour come   965
    back,
  I could prevent this storm and shun thy wrack!

967. **lackey:** servile follower.

968. **cross:** thwart.

975. **bedrid:** bedridden.

981. **curled hair:** probably meant as a mark of vanity.

985. **orts:** food scraps, leavings.

993. **unrecalling:** unrecallable.

"At his own shadow let the thief run mad,
Himself himself seek every hour to kill!"
From Whitney's emblem of a man running from his conscience,
in *A Choice of Emblems* (1586).

"Thou ceaseless lackey to eternity,
With some mischance cross Tarquin in his flight;
Devise extremes beyond extremity,
To make him curse this cursed crimeful night;   970
Let ghastly shadows his lewd eyes affright,
    And the dire thought of his committed evil
    Shape every bush a hideous shapeless devil.

"Disturb his hours of rest with restless trances,
Afflict him in his bed with bedrid groans;   975
Let there bechance him pitiful mischances,
To make him moan, but pity not his moans.
Stone him with hardened hearts, harder than stones;
    And let mild women to him lose their mildness,
    Wilder to him than tigers in their wildness.   980

"Let him have time to tear his curled hair,
Let him have time against himself to rave,
Let him have time of time's help to despair,
Let him have time to live a loathed slave,
Let him have time a beggar's orts to crave,   985
    And time to see one that by alms doth live
    Disdain to him disdained scraps to give.

"Let him have time to see his friends his foes,
And merry fools to mock at him resort;
Let him have time to mark how slow time goes   990
In time of sorrow, and how swift and short
His time of folly and his time of sport;
    And ever let his unrecalling crime
    Have time to wail th'abusing of his time.

998. **Himself himself . . . to kill:** let him seek every hour to kill himself.

1001. **sland'rous:** despicable; **deathsman:** executioner.

1003. **hope:** future.

1007. **presently:** immediately; this word has deteriorated in meaning over the years.

1008. **them:** themselves; **list:** choose.

1013. **grooms:** servants; **sightless night:** hidden in darkness; the meaning of the line is that servants remain hidden in obscurity but kings are as conspicuous as bright daylight.

1017. **arbitrators:** settlers of disputes.

1018. **in skill-contending schools:** among schoolmen who dispute for the sake of disputing.

1021. **I force not argument a straw:** I don't give a straw for argument.

"But if the like the snow-white swan desire,
The stain upon his silver down will stay."
From George Vertue, *A Description of the Works of . . . Wenceslaus Hollar* (1759).

"O Time, thou tutor both to good and bad,   995
Teach me to curse him that thou taught'st this ill!
At his own shadow let the thief run mad,
Himself himself seek every hour to kill!
Such wretched hands such wretched blood should
     spill;
     For who so base would such an office have   1000
     As sland'rous deathsman to so base a slave?

"The baser is he, coming from a king,
To shame his hope with deeds degenerate.
The mightier man, the mightier is the thing
That makes him honored or begets him hate;   1005
For greatest scandal waits on greatest state.
     The moon being clouded presently is missed,
     But little stars may hide them when they list.

"The crow may bathe his coal-black wings in mire
And unperceived fly with the filth away;   1010
But if the like the snow-white swan desire,
The stain upon his silver down will stay.
Poor grooms are sightless night, kings glorious day.
     Gnats are unnoted wheresoe'er they fly,
     But eagles gazed upon with every eye.   1015

"Out, idle words, servants to shallow fools!
Unprofitable sounds, weak arbitrators!
Busy yourselves in skill-contending schools;
Debate where leisure serves with dull debaters;
To trembling clients be you mediators.   1020
     For me, I force not argument a straw,
     Since that my case is past the help of law.

1025. **cavil with:** quibble about.
1026. **confirmed despite:** assured shame.
1027. **helpless:** unhelpful.
1037. **betumbled:** disordered.
1039. **imparteth:** supplies.
1050. **rifled:** robbed.

"Gnats are unnoted wheresoe'er they fly,
But eagles gazed upon with every eye."
From Konrad Gesner, *Historia animalium* (1585).

"In vain I rail at Opportunity,
At Time, at Tarquin, and uncheerful Night;
In vain I cavil with mine infamy,   1025
In vain I spurn at my confirmed despite:
This helpless smoke of words doth me no right.
  The remedy indeed to do me good
  Is to let forth my foul-defiled blood.

"Poor hand, why quiver'st thou at this decree?   1030
Honor thyself to rid me of this shame;
For if I die, my honor lives in thee,
But if I live, thou livest in my defame.
Since thou couldst not defend thy loyal dame
  And wast afeard to scratch her wicked foe,   1035
  Kill both thyself and her for yielding so."

This said, from her betumbled couch she starteth,
To find some desp'rate instrument of death.
But this no slaughterhouse no tool imparteth
To make more vent for passage of her breath,   1040
Which, thronging through her lips, so vanisheth
  As smoke from Etna that in air consumes,
  Or that which from discharged cannon fumes.

"In vain," quoth she, "I live, and seek in vain
Some happy mean to end a hapless life.   1045
I feared by Tarquin's falchion to be slain,
Yet for the selfsame purpose seek a knife;
But when I feared I was a loyal wife;
  So am I now—O no, that cannot be;
  Of that true type hath Tarquin rifled me.   1050

1054. **A badge . . . livery:** the metaphor refers to the badge worn on the sleeve of a servant in Shakespeare's time showing his master's device or crest. A modern equivalent might be the distinguishing badges of various units of the armed forces.

1061. **infringed:** violated.

1062. **graff:** offshoot of another stock that has been grafted.

1070. **dispense:** atone for; pardon in the sense of a papal dispensation.

1074. **sable ground:** heraldic term for a black background or field for a coat-of-arms.

1077. **dale:** valley.

"O, that is gone for which I sought to live,
And therefore now I need not fear to die.
To clear this spot by death, at least I give
A badge of fame to slander's livery,
A dying life to living infamy.   1055
    Poor helpless help, the treasure stol'n away,
    To burn the guiltless casket where it lay!

"Well, well, dear Collatine, thou shalt not know
The stained taste of violated troth;
I will not wrong thy true affection so,   1060
To flatter thee with an infringed oath;
This bastard graff shall never come to growth;
    He shall not boast who did thy stock pollute
    That thou art doting father of his fruit.

"Nor shall he smile at thee in secret thought,   1065
Nor laugh with his companions at thy state;
But thou shalt know thy int'rest was not bought
Basely with gold, but stol'n from forth thy gate.
For me, I am the mistress of my fate,
    And with my trespass never will dispense,   1070
    Till life to death acquit my forced offence.

"I will not poison thee with my attaint,
Nor fold my fault in cleanly-coined excuses;
My sable ground of sin I will not paint
To hide the truth of this false night's abuses.   1075
My tongue shall utter all; mine eyes, like sluices,
    As from a mountain spring that feeds a dale,
    Shall gush pure streams to purge my impure tale."

1079. Philomel: Philomela, in Greek mythology, was forced to marry her sister's husband, who cut out Philomela's tongue to silence her. She told her story in writing and was changed by the gods into a swallow. In Roman mythology, she was turned into a nightingale, and *Philomel* became the poetic name for the nightingale.

1094. fond and testy: foolish and ill-humored.

Tereus cutting out the tongue of Philomela so she could not tell that he had ravished her. From Gabriele Simeoni, *Vita et Metamorfoseo d'Ovidio* (1559).

By this, lamenting Philomel had ended
The well-tuned warble of her nightly sorrow,   1080
And solemn night with slow sad gait descended
To ugly hell; when lo, the blushing morrow
Lends light to all fair eyes that light will borrow;
   But cloudy Lucrece shames herself to see,
   And therefore still in night would cloistered be.   1085

Revealing day through every cranny spies,
And seems to point her out where she sits weeping;
To whom she sobbing speaks: "O eye of eyes,
Why pry'st thou through my window? Leave thy
    peeping;
Mock with thy tickling beams eyes that are sleeping;   1090
   Brand not my forehead with thy piercing light,
   For day hath nought to do what's done by night."

Thus cavils she with every thing she sees.
True grief is fond and testy as a child,
Who wayward once, his mood with nought agrees.   1095
Old woes, not infant sorrows, bear them mild;
Continuance tames the one; the other wild,
   Like an unpracticed swimmer plunging still
   With too much labor drowns for want of skill.

So she, deep-drenched in a sea of care,   1100
Holds disputation with each thing she views,
And to herself all sorrow doth compare;
No object but her passion's strength renews,
And as one shifts, another straight ensues.
   Sometime her grief is dumb and hath no words;   1105
   Sometime 'tis mad and too much talk affords.

1109. **search the bottom of annoy:** reach the very depths of irritation.

1113. **When . . . sympathized:** when it is brought together with a similar grief.

1114. **in ken of:** in sight of.

1126. **Relish . . . ears:** give pleasure with your ditties to ears that will be pleased.

1127. **dumps:** melancholy songs.

1132. **diapason:** harmony.

1133. **For burden-wise . . . still:** For, with a continued refrain, I'll go on about Tarquin.

1134. **Tereus:** Thracian prince who ravished Philomela; **descants:** sings.

The little birds that tune their morning's joy
Make her moans mad with their sweet melody;
For mirth doth search the bottom of annoy;
Sad souls are slain in merry company;   1110
Grief best is pleased with grief's society.
  True sorrow then is feelingly suffized
  When with like semblance it is sympathized.

'Tis double death to drown in ken of shore;
He ten times pines that pines beholding food;   1115
To see the salve doth make the wound ache more;
Great grief grieves most at that would do it good;
Deep woes roll forward like a gentle flood,
  Who, being stopped, the bounding banks o'erflows;
  Grief dallied with nor law nor limit knows.   1120

"You mocking birds," quoth she, "your tunes entomb
Within your hollow-swelling feathered breasts,
And in my hearing be you mute and dumb.
My restless discord loves no stops nor rests;
A woeful hostess brooks not merry guests.   1125
  Relish your nimble notes to pleasing ears;
  Distress likes dumps when time is kept with tears.

"Come, Philomel, that sing'st of ravishment,
Make thy sad grove in my disheveled hair.
As the dank earth weeps at thy languishment,   1130
So I at each sad strain will strain a tear,
And with deep groans the diapason bear;
  For burden-wise I'll hum on Tarquin still,
  While thou on Tereus descants better skill.

1135. **against a thorn:** in Shakespeare's time it was believed, at least by poets, that the nightingale's song was mournful because when it sang it leaned against a thorn that pierced its breast.

1140. **frets:** ridges on the fingerboard of a stringed musical instrument.

1141. **languishment:** condition of pining in sorrow.

1143. **As shaming:** for shame that.

1144. **seated from the way:** situated in an out-of-the-way place.

1147. **creatures stern:** wild animals; **kinds:** qualities.

1153. **in mutiny:** in doubt.

1156-57. **To kill . . . pollution:** Lucrece debates as to whether she should damn her soul by killing her body.

A "winding maze" or labyrinth. From Claude Menestrier, *L'art des emblemes* (1684).

"And whiles against a thorn thou bear'st thy part   1135
To keep thy sharp woes waking, wretched I,
To imitate thee well, against my heart
Will fix a sharp knife to affright mine eye;
Who, if it wink, shall thereon fall and die.
   These means, as frets upon an instrument,   1140
   Shall tune our heartstrings to true languishment.

"And for, poor bird, thou sing'st not in the day,
As shaming any eye should thee behold,
Some dark deep desert, seated from the way,
That knows not parching heat nor freezing cold,   1145
Will we find out; and there we will unfold
   To creatures stern sad tunes, to change their kinds.
   Since men prove beasts, let beasts bear gentle
     minds."

As the poor frighted deer, that stands at gaze,
Wildly determining which way to fly,   1150
Or one encompassed with a winding maze
That cannot tread the way out readily;
So with herself is she in mutiny,
   To live or die which of the twain were better,
   When life is shamed and death reproach's debtor. 1155

"To kill myself," quoth she, "alack, what were it,
But with my body my poor soul's pollution?
They that lose half with greater patience bear it
Than they whose whole is swallowed in confusion.
That mother tries a merciless conclusion   1160

1167. **pilled:** peeled.
1183. **writ in my testament:** written in my will.

Who, having two sweet babes, when death takes
   one,
Will slay the other and be nurse to none.

"My body or my soul, which was the dearer,
When the one pure, the other made divine?
Whose love of either to myself was nearer,   1165
When both were kept for heaven and Collatine?
Ay me! The bark pilled from the lofty pine,
   His leaves will wither and his sap decay;
   So must my soul, her bark being pilled away.

"Her house is sacked, her quiet interrupted,   1170
Her mansion battered by the enemy;
Her sacred temple spotted, spoiled, corrupted,
Grossly engirt with daring infamy;
Then let it not be called impiety
   If in this blemished fort I make some hole   1175
   Through which I may convey this troubled soul.

"Yet die I will not till my Collatine
Have heard the cause of my untimely death,
That he may vow, in that sad hour of mine,
Revenge on him that made me stop my breath.   1180
My stained blood to Tarquin I'll bequeath,
   Which by him tainted shall for him be spent,
   And as his due writ in my testament.

"My honor I'll bequeath unto the knife
That wounds my body so dishonored.   1185
'Tis honor to deprive dishonored life;

1191. **jewel:** chastity.
1198. **abridgment:** alteration.
1202. **confound:** ruin.
1203. **disbursed be:** be paid.
1206. **overseen:** fooled.
1207. **ill:** disgrace.
1213. **brinish pearl:** tear.

The one will live, the other being dead.
So of shame's ashes shall my fame be bred;
  For in my death I murder shameful scorn.
  My shame so dead, mine honor is newborn.   1190

"Dear lord of that dear jewel I have lost,
What legacy shall I bequeath to thee?
My resolution, love, shall be thy boast,
By whose example thou revenged mayst be.
How Tarquin must be used, read it in me: 1195
  Myself, thy friend, will kill myself, thy foe,
  And, for my sake, serve thou false Tarquin so.

"This brief abridgment of my will I make:
My soul and body to the skies and ground;
My resolution, husband, do thou take;   1200
Mine honor be the knife's that makes my wound;
My shame be his that did my fame confound;
  And all my fame that lives disbursed be
  To those that live and think no shame of me.

"Thou, Collatine, shalt oversee this will;   1205
How was I overseen that thou shalt see it!
My blood shall wash the slander of mine ill;
My life's foul deed, my life's fair end shall free it.
Faint not, faint heart, but stoutly say 'So be it'.
  Yield to my hand; my hand shall conquer thee;   1210
  Thou dead, both die and both shall victors be."

This plot of death when sadly she had laid,
And wiped the brinish pearl from her bright eyes,
With untuned tongue she hoarsely calls her maid,

1215. **hies:** runs.

1218. **meads:** fields.

1221. **sorts:** adapts.

1223. **audaciously:** boldly.

1224. **two suns:** two eyes.

1226-27. **But . . . eye:** dew forming at night on the flowers.

1234. **ivory conduits:** white fountains; **coral cisterns:** red eyes.

1238. **smarts:** hurts.

"As winter meads when sun doth melt their snow."
From Whitney's *A Choice of Emblems* (1586).

Whose swift obedience to her mistress hies;   1215
For fleet-winged duty with thought's feathers flies.
   Poor Lucrece' cheeks unto her maid seem so
   As winter meads when sun doth melt their snow.

Her mistress she doth give demure good morrow
With soft slow tongue, true mark of modesty,   1220
And sorts a sad look to her lady's sorrow,
For why her face wore sorrow's livery,
But durst not ask of her audaciously
   Why her two suns were cloud-eclipsèd so,
   Nor why her fair cheeks overwashed with woe.   1225

But as the earth doth weep, the sun being set,
Each flower moistened like a melting eye,
Even so the maid with swelling drops 'gan wet
Her circled eyne, enforced by sympathy
Of those fair suns set in her mistress' sky,   1230
   Who in a salt-waved ocean quench their light,
   Which makes the maid weep like the dewy night.

A pretty while these pretty creatures stand,
Like ivory conduits coral cisterns filling.
One justly weeps; the other takes in hand   1235
No cause but company of her drops spilling:
Their gentle sex to weep are often willing,
   Grieving themselves to guess at others' smarts,
   And then they drown their eyes or break their
     hearts.

For men have marble, women waxen, minds,   1240
And therefore are they formed as marble will;

1242. **kinds:** traits.

1247. **champaign plain:** level field.

1251. **mote:** tiny speck.

1247-53. The sense of this stanza is expressed in the last two lines: women's faces are smooth and unable to hide secrets whereas men's faces are rough and capable of concealment.

1254. **inveigh:** complain.

1257. **hild:** held.

1258. **fulfilled:** completely filled.

1261. **precedent:** example.

1265-67. **Such danger . . . body dead:** Lucrece rejects suicide because she fears that being dead false reports might tarnish her memory.

1269. **poor counterfeit . . . complaining:** to the poor image of her own sorrow; in other words, her grieving maid.

The weak oppressed, th'impression of strange kinds
Is formed in them by force, by fraud, or skill.
Then call them not the authors of their ill,
   No more than wax shall be accounted evil   1245
   Wherein is stamped the semblance of a devil.

Their smoothness, like a goodly champaign plain,
Lays open all the little worms that creep;
In men, as in a rough-grown grove, remain
Cave-keeping evils that obscurely sleep.   1250
Through crystal walls each little mote will peep.
   Though men can cover crimes with bold stern looks,
   Poor women's faces are their own faults' books.

No man inveigh against the withered flower,
But chide rough winter that the flower hath killed.   1255
Not that devoured, but that which doth devour,
Is worthy blame. O, let it not be hild
Poor women's faults that they are so fulfilled
   With men's abuses: those proud lords to blame
   Make weak-made women tenants to their shame.   1260

The precedent whereof in Lucrece view,
Assailed by night with circumstances strong
Of present death, and shame that might ensue
By that her death, to do her husband wrong.
Such danger to resistance did belong,   1265
   That dying fear through all her body spread;
   And who cannot abuse a body dead?

By this, mild patience bid fair Lucrece speak
To the poor counterfeit of her complaining.

1272. **of my sustaining:** that I endure.

1273. **small avails my mood:** little helps my grief.

1278. **sluggard:** lazy.

1279. **dispense:** make excuse.

1283. **heaviness:** sadness.

1285. **repetition:** repeating of it.

"My girl," quoth she, "on what occasion break   1270
Those tears from thee that down thy cheeks are
    raining?
If thou dost weep for grief of my sustaining,
    Know, gentle wench, it small avails my mood;
    If tears could help, mine own would do me good.

"But tell me, girl, when went"—and there she stayed 1275
Till after a deep groan—"Tarquin from hence?"
"Madam, ere I was up," replied the maid,
"The more to blame my sluggard negligence.
Yet with the fault I thus far can dispense:
    Myself was stirring ere the break of day,   1280
    And ere I rose was Tarquin gone away.

"But, lady, if your maid may be so bold,
She would request to know your heaviness."
"O, peace!" quoth Lucrece: "if it should be told,
The repetition cannot make it less,   1285
For more it is than I can well express;
    And that deep torture may be called a hell
    When more is felt than one hath power to tell.

"Go, get me hither paper, ink and pen;
Yet save that labor, for I have them here.   1290
What should I say? One of my husband's men
Bid thou be ready by and by to bear
A letter to my lord, my love, my dear.
    Bid him with speed prepare to carry it;
    The cause craves haste and it will soon be writ."   1295

1298. **Conceit:** thinking.

1299. **will:** intense feeling.

1300. **curious-good:** intricate; fancifully expressed.

1302. **inventions:** constructions.

1310. **tenure:** legal term for a certified and true transcript.

1312. **schedule:** scroll of writing.

1313. **quality:** cause.

1317. **passion:** emotion.

Her maid is gone, and she prepares to write,
First hovering o'er the paper with her quill.
Conceit and grief an eager combat fight;
What wit sets down is blotted straight with will;
This is too curious-good, this blunt and ill:　　　　1300
　　Much like a press of people at a door,
　　Throng her inventions, which shall go before.

At last she thus begins: "Thou worthy lord
Of that unworthy wife that greeteth thee,
Health to thy person! Next vouchsafe t'afford—　　1305
If ever, love, thy Lucrece thou wilt see—
Some present speed to come and visit me.
　　So I commend me, from our house in grief;
　　My woes are tedious, though my words are brief."

Here folds she up the tenure of her woe,　　　　1310
Her certain sorrow writ uncertainly.
By this short schedule Collatine may know
Her grief, but not her grief's true quality;
She dares not thereof make discovery,
　　Lest he should hold it her own gross abuse,　　1315
　　Ere she with blood had stained her stained excuse.

Besides, the life and feeling of her passion
She hoards, to spend when he is by to hear her,
When sighs and groans and tears may grace the
　　　　fashion
Of her disgrace, the better so to clear her　　　　1320
From that suspicion which the world might bear her.
　　To shun this blot, she would not blot the letter
　　With words, till action might become them better.

1329. **sounds:** waters.

1333. **post attends:** messenger waits.

1335. **lagging fowls . . . blast:** late-migrating birds before the winter winds from the north.

1336-37. **Speed . . . extremes:** these lines appear to mean that her extreme desire for speed makes her think that such speed as can be attained is dull and slow and she demands still greater haste.

1338. **homely villain:** kindly servant.

1340. **or yea or no:** either yea or no.

1345. **silly groom:** simple servant; **God wot:** God knows.

1350. **pattern . . . age:** example from an age that is past.

1351. **Pawned:** gave; **gage:** promise.

Troy attacked by "the power of Greece," sixteenth-century style. From Isaac de la Rivière, *Speculum heroici* (1613).

100

To see sad sights moves more than hear them told;
For then the eye interprets to the ear   1325
The heavy motion that it doth behold,
When every part a part of woe doth bear.
'Tis but a part of sorrow that we hear:
  Deep sounds make lesser noise than shallow fords,
  And sorrow ebbs, being blown with wind of words. 1330

Her letter now is sealed and on it writ
"At Ardea to my lord with more than haste."
The post attends, and she delivers it,
Charging the sour-faced groom to hie as fast
As lagging fowls before the northern blast.   1335
  Speed more than speed but dull and slow she
    deems:
  Extremity still urgeth such extremes.

The homely villain curtsies to her low,
And blushing on her, with a steadfast eye
Receives the scroll without or yea or no,   1340
And forth with bashful innocence doth hie.
But they whose guilt within their bosoms lie
  Imagine every eye beholds their blame;
  For Lucrece thought he blushed to see her shame:

When, silly groom, God wot, it was defect   1345
Of spirit, life and bold audacity.
Such harmless creatures have a true respect
To talk in deeds, while others saucily
Promise more speed but do it leisurely.
  Even so this pattern of the worn-out age   1350
  Pawned honest looks, but laid no words to gage.

1355. **wistly**: knowingly.

1356. **earnest**: severe.

1361. **entertain**: occupy.

1364. **plaints**: lamentations; **stay**: curtail.

1367. **Priam**: King of Troy.

1368. **power**: army.

1370. **Ilion**: poetical name for Troy.

1371. **conceited**: skillful.

1377. **strife**: effort.

"Bold Hector" and Ajax. From Whitney's *A Choice of Emblems* (1586).

His kindled duty kindled her mistrust,
That two red fires in both their faces blazed;
She thought he blushed, as knowing Tarquin's lust,
And blushing with him, wistly on him gazed; 1355
Her earnest eye did make him more amazed;
  The more she saw the blood his cheeks replenish,
  The more she thought he spied in her some blemish.

But long she thinks till he return again,
And yet the duteous vassal scarce is gone. 1360
The weary time she cannot entertain,
For now 'tis stale to sigh, to weep and groan;
So woe hath wearied woe, moan tired moan,
  That she her plaints a little while doth stay,
  Pausing for means to mourn some newer way. 1365

At last she calls to mind where hangs a piece
Of skillful painting, made for Priam's Troy,
Before the which is drawn the power of Greece,
For Helen's rape the city to destroy,
Threat'ning cloud-kissing Ilion with annoy; 1370
  Which the conceited painter drew so proud
  As heaven, it seemed, to kiss the turrets bowed.

A thousand lamentable objects there,
In scorn of nature, art gave lifeless life:
Many a dry drop seemed a weeping tear, 1375
Shed for the slaughtered husband by the wife;
The red blood reeked, to show the painter's strife;
  And dying eyes gleamed forth their ashy lights,
  Like dying coals burnt out in tedious nights.

1380. **pioneer:** soldier assigned to tunneling and digging.

1384. **lust:** pleasure.

1392. **heartless:** disheartened; cowardly.

1394. **Ajax:** one of the Greek heroes in Homer's *Iliad;* **Ulysses:** another of the Greek warriors.

1394-95. **art/Of physiognomy:** art of reading a person's character in his countenance.

1396. **ciphered:** revealed; literally written out.

1400. **government:** control.

1401. **Nestor:** oldest and wisest of the Greeks.

1404. **beguiled:** attracted.

1407. **purled:** flowed.

"As if some mermaid did their ears entice"
Mermaids were known for the irresistible music with which they lured ancient mariners to rocky shores and their doom. On the shore are two harpies, more directly associated with death. From Cartari's *Imagini* (1609).

There might you see the laboring pioneer   1380
Begrimed with sweat and smeared all with dust;
And from the towers of Troy there would appear
The very eyes of men through loopholes thrust,
Gazing upon the Greeks with little lust.
  Such sweet observance in this work was had   1385
  That one might see those far-off eyes look sad.

In great commanders grace and majesty
You might behold, triumphing in their faces;
In youth, quick bearing and dexterity;
And here and there the painter interlaces   1390
Pale cowards marching on with trembling paces,
  Which heartless peasants did so well resemble
  That one would swear he saw them quake and
    tremble.

In Ajax and Ulysses, O what art
Of physiognomy might one behold!   1395
The face of either ciphered either's heart;
Their face their manners most expressly told:
In Ajax' eyes blunt rage and rigor rolled;
  But the mild glance that sly Ulysses lent
  Showed deep regard and smiling government.   1400

There pleading might you see grave Nestor stand,
As 'twere encouraging the Greeks to fight,
Making such sober action with his hand
That it beguiled attention, charmed the sight.
In speech, it seemed, his beard all silver white   1405
  Wagged up and down, and from his lips did fly
  Thin winding breath which purled up to the sky.

1410. **graces:** with different appearances of interest.

1412. **nice:** exact.

1417. **thronged:** crowded; **bears:** pushes; **boll'n:** swollen.

1418. **pelt:** clamor.

1424. **Achilles:** reputedly the bravest of the Greeks.

1425. **Griped:** gripped.

1430. **Hector:** the champion of the Trojan forces.

1433. **odd action yield:** strange attitudes display.

1435. **heavy fear:** melancholy fear.

Impar Priamides dio congressus Achilli,
Strato cæsus Hector ab hoste cadit: 22.
Raptatur, agit circum sua mœnia curru,
Heu decus Iliaci splendor et imperij.

Hector falls at the hand of Achilles. From de la Rivière, *Speculum* (1613).

About him were a press of gaping faces,
Which seemed to swallow up his sound advice,
All jointly list'ning, but with several graces,   1410
As if some mermaid did their ears entice,
Some high, some low, the painter was so nice;
  The scalps of many, almost hid behind,
  To jump up higher seemed, to mock the mind.

Here one man's hand leaned on another's head,   1415
His nose being shadowed by his neighbor's ear;
Here one being thronged bears back, all boll'n and
    red;
Another smothered seems to pelt and swear;
And in their rage such signs of rage they bear
  As, but for loss of Nestor's golden words,   1420
  It seemed they would debate with angry swords.

For much imaginary work was there;
Conceit deceitful, so compact, so kind,
That for Achilles' image stood his spear
Griped in an armed hand; himself behind   1425
Was left unseen, save to the eye of mind:
  A hand, a foot, a face, a leg, a head,
  Stood for the whole to be imagined.

And from the walls of strong-besieged Troy
When their brave hope, bold Hector, marched to field, 1430
Stood many Trojan mothers sharing joy
To see their youthful sons bright weapons wield;
And to their hope they such odd action yield
  That through their light joy seemed to appear,
  Like bright things stained, a kind of heavy fear.   1435

1436. **strond of Dardan:** strand (shore) of Dardania, another name for the country of Troas in which Troy was situated.

1437. **Simois:** river that flows into the plain of Troy.

1440. **galled:** waterworn; **than:** then.

1444. **stelled:** contained.

1446. **dolor:** grief.

1447. **Hecuba:** wife of Priam.

1449. **Pyrrhus:** another name for Neoptolemus, the Greek warrior who killed Priam.

1450. **anatomized:** dissected.

1452. **chops:** seams.

1453. **semblance:** resemblance.

1455. **pipes:** veins.

1457. **spends her eyes:** gazes with fixed attention.

1458. **beldam's:** old woman's.

1459. **wants:** lacks.

Pyrrhus and "despairing Hecuba." From Ovid, *Metamorphoses* (1565).

104

And from the strond of Dardan where they fought
To Simois' reedy banks the red blood ran,
Whose waves to imitate the battle sought
With swelling ridges; and their ranks began
To break upon the galled shore, and than   1440
  Retire again, till meeting greater ranks
  They join and shoot their foam at Simois' banks.

To this well-painted piece is Lucrece come,
To find a face where all distress is stelled.
Many she sees where cares have carved some,   1445
But none where all distress and dolor dwelled,
Till she despairing Hecuba beheld,
  Staring on Priam's wounds with her old eyes,
  Which bleeding under Pyrrhus' proud foot lies.

In her the painter had anatomized   1450
Time's ruin, beauty's wrack, and grim care's reign;
Her cheeks with chops and wrinkles were disguised;
Of what she was no semblance did remain;
Her blue blood changed to black in every vein,
  Wanting the spring that those shrunk pipes had 1455
    fed,
  Showed life imprisoned in a body dead.

On this sad shadow Lucrece spends her eyes,
And shapes her sorrow to the beldam's woes,
Who nothing wants to answer her but cries,
And bitter words to ban her cruel foes: 1460
The painter was no god to lend her those;
  And therefore Lucrece swears he did her wrong,
  To give her so much grief and not a tongue.

1465. **tune thy woes:** sing thy sorrows.

1471. **strumpet:** Helen; **stir:** tumult.

1476. **trespass:** offense.

1479. **moe:** more.

1484. **To plague . . . in general:** why should the whole group suffer to atone for a private sin.

1486. **Troilus:** another Trojan hero; **swounds:** swoons, faints.

1487. **channel:** trench.

1488. **And friend . . . wounds:** friends wound each other in ignorance of identity; Troy was sacked at night.

"Poor instrument," quoth she, "without a sound,
I'll tune thy woes with my lamenting tongue,   1465
And drop sweet balm in Priam's painted wound,
And rail on Pyrrhus that hath done him wrong,
And with my tears quench Troy that burns so long,
  And with my knife scratch out the angry eyes
  Of all the Greeks that are thine enemies.   1470

"Show me the strumpet that began this stir,
That with my nails her beauty I may tear.
Thy heat of lust, fond Paris, did incur
This load of wrath that burning Troy doth bear.
Thy eye kindled the fire that burneth here;   1475
  And here in Troy, for trespass of thine eye,
  The sire, the son, the dame and daughter die.

"Why should the private pleasure of some one
Become the public plague of many moe?
Let sin, alone committed, light alone   1480
Upon his head that hath transgressed so;
Let guiltless souls be freed from guilty woe.
  For one's offence why should so many fall,
  To plague a private sin in general?

"Lo, here weeps Hecuba, here Priam dies,   1485
Here manly Hector faints, here Troilus swounds,
Here friend by friend in bloody channel lies,
And friend to friend gives unadvised wounds,
And one man's lust these many lives confounds.
  Had doting Priam checked his son's desire,   1490
  Troy had been bright with fame and not with fire."

1492. **Troy's painted woes:** Troy's sufferings as depicted in the painting.

1497. **penciled:** drawn (by the artist's pencil); **pensiveness:** soberness.

1499. **She throws . . . round:** she looks the whole painting over.

1500. **forlorn:** wretched; in a pitiful plight.

1501. **image:** individual.

1502. **That . . . lent:** that made the Phrygian shepherds look with pity.

1504. **blunt swains:** dull countrymen.

1509. **brow unbent:** unfrowning.

1511. **instance:** evidence.

1513-14. **But, like . . . just:** Shakespeare here begins a description of Sinon, the Greek who treacherously persuaded the Trojans to take in the wooden horse in which Greek soldiers were hidden. This story is taken from Virgil's *Aeneid*, II, 13-267.

1514. **entertained:** supported.

1515. **ensconced:** concealed.

1516. **jealousy:** distrust; **mistrust:** suspect.

1517. **creeping craft:** sly cunning; **perjury:** lying.

Here feelingly she weeps Troy's painted woes;
For sorrow, like a heavy-hanging bell
Once set on ringing, with his own weight goes;
Then little strength rings out the doleful knell;   1495
So Lucrece, set a-work, sad tales doth tell
　　To penciled pensiveness and colored sorrow;
　　She lends them words, and she their looks doth
　　　borrow.

She throws her eyes about the painting round,
And who she finds forlorn she doth lament.   1500
At last she sees a wretched image bound
That piteous looks to Phrygian shepherds lent;
His face, though full of cares, yet showed content;
　　Onward to Troy with the blunt swains he goes,
　　So mild that Patience seemed to scorn his woes.   1505

In him the painter labored with his skill
To hide deceit and give the harmless show
An humble gait, calm looks, eyes wailing still,
A brow unbent that seemed to welcome woe;
Cheeks neither red nor pale, but mingled so   1510
　　That blushing red no guilty instance gave,
　　Nor ashy pale the fear that false hearts have.

But, like a constant and confirmed devil,
He entertained a show so seeming just,
And therein so ensconced his secret evil,   1515
That jealousy itself could not mistrust
False creeping craft and perjury should thrust
　　Into so bright a day such black-faced storms,
　　Or blot with hell-born sin such saintlike forms.

1521-22. **whose . . . slew:** the treacherous story that Sinon told resulted in Priam's death.

1526. **glass:** mirror; Shakespeare pictures Troy as a mirror in which the stars saw themselves reflected.

1527. **advisedly:** contemplatively.

1528. **chid:** reproved.

1529-30. **Saying . . . ill:** saying that he had used some other person as a model for false Sinon because so handsome a person as that pictured could not harbor a mind so evil.

1533. **belied:** false.

1534. **guile:** evil.

1536. **the while:** on the instant.

1539. **turned it thus:** changed the meaning in this fashion.

1543. **travail:** labor.

1544. **to beguild:** this phrase has been the subject of much speculation as to its meaning. *Beguild* may be an old variant form of "beguile." Edmond Malone in the eighteenth century suggested that *to* ought to be emended to "so." Perhaps the meaning is simply "to beguile"; Malone's suggestion that the phrase means "so beguiled" is tempting.

"Perjured Sinon" smiles to see Troy burn. From Whitney's *A Choice of Emblems* (1586).

The well-skilled workman this mild image drew   1520
For perjured Sinon, whose enchanting story
The credulous old Priam after slew;
Whose words, like wildfire, burnt the shining glory
Of rich-built Ilion, that the skies were sorry,
    And little stars shot from their fixed places,   1525
    When their glass fell wherein they viewed their
      faces.

This picture she advisedly perused,
And chid the painter for his wondrous skill,
Saying, some shape in Sinon's was abused;
So fair a form lodged not a mind so ill;   1530
And still on him she gazed, and gazing still
    Such signs of truth in his plain face she spied
    That she concludes the picture was belied.

"It cannot be," quoth she, "that so much guile"—
She would have said "can lurk in such a look";   1535
But Tarquin's shape came in her mind the while,
And from her tongue "can lurk" from "cannot" took;
"It cannot be" she in that sense forsook,
    And turned it thus, "It cannot be, I find,
    But such a face should bear a wicked mind.   1540

"For even as subtle Sinon here is painted,
So sober-sad, so weary and so mild,
As if with grief or travail he had fainted,
To me came Tarquin armed to beguild
With outward honesty, but yet defiled   1545
    With inward vice. As Priam him did cherish,
    So did I Tarquin; so my Troy did perish.

1549. **borrowed:** faked.

1551. **falls:** drops.

1562. **passion:** emotion.

1564. **senseless:** inanimate.

1567. **gives o'er:** ceases.

1573. **Short time . . . sustaining:** a short time seems long because of the keen sorrow she endures.

"Look, look, how list'ning Priam wets his eyes,
To see those borrowed tears that Sinon sheds.
Priam, why art thou old and yet not wise?   1550
For every tear he falls a Trojan bleeds;
His eye drops fire, no water thence proceeds;
    Those round clear pearls of his that move thy pity
    Are balls of quenchless fire to burn thy city.

"Such devils steal effects from lightless hell;   1555
For Sinon in his fire doth quake with cold,
And in that cold hot-burning fire doth dwell;
These contraries such unity do hold
Only to flatter fools and make them bold;
    So Priam's trust false Sinon's tears doth flatter   1560
    That he finds means to burn his Troy with water."

Here, all enraged, such passion her assails,
That patience is quite beaten from her breast.
She tears the senseless Sinon with her nails,
Comparing him to that unhappy guest   1565
Whose deed hath made herself herself detest.
    At last she smilingly with this gives o'er:
    "Fool, fool!" quoth she. "His wounds will not be
        sore."

Thus ebbs and flows the current of her sorrow,
And time doth weary time with her complaining.   1570
She looks for night, and then she longs for morrow,
And both she thinks too long with her remaining.
Short time seems long in sorrow's sharp sustaining;
    Though woe be heavy, yet it seldom sleeps,
    And they that watch see time how slow it creeps.   1575

1576. **overslipped her thought:** gone unnoticed.

1579. **surmise:** contemplation; **detriment:** misfortunes.

1580. **discontent:** unhappiness.

1583. **mindful:** trustworthy.

1586. **distained:** stained.

1588. **water galls:** faint rim, or secondary rainbow, that sometimes circles a vivid rainbow; **dim element:** darkened sky.

1592. **sod:** steeped.

1596. **chance:** fortune; condition.

1598. **uncouth:** mysterious; strange.

1600. **spite:** calamity.

1601. **attired in discontent:** covered with unhappiness.

1602. **Unmask . . . heaviness:** reveal this sad grief.

Which all this time hath overslipped her thought
That she with painted images hath spent,
Being from the feeling of her own grief brought
By deep surmise of others' detriment,
Losing her woes in shows of discontent.   1580
  It easeth some, though none it ever cured,
  To think their dolor others have endured.

But now the mindful messenger come back
Brings home his lord and other company;
Who finds his Lucrece clad in mourning black,   1585
And round about her tear-distained eye
Blue circles streamed, like rainbows in the sky.
  These water galls in her dim element
  Foretell new storms to those already spent.

Which when her sad-beholding husband saw,   1590
Amazedly in her sad face he stares:
Her eyes, though sod in tears, looked red and raw,
Her lively color killed with deadly cares.
He hath no power to ask her how she fares;
  Both stood, like old acquaintance in a trance,   1595
  Met far from home, wond'ring each other's chance.

At last he takes her by the bloodless hand,
And thus begins: "What uncouth ill event
Hath thee befall'n, that thou dost trembling stand?
Sweet love, what spite hath thy fair color spent?   1600
Why art thou thus attired in discontent?
  Unmask, dear dear, this moody heaviness,
  And tell thy grief, that we may give redress."

1604-5. **Three times . . . woe:** the metaphor here is from the igniting of a fuse to fire a musket. Lucrece *gives . . . fire* (lights the fuse) three times before she can discharge her words of woe.

1609. **consorted lords:** retinue.

1612. **certain:** inevitable.

1614. **give . . . amending:** correct the fault.

1615. **depending:** threatening.

1619. **in . . . bed:** perhaps "in the hope of sharing."

1621. **wast wont:** were accustomed.

1631. **contradict:** refuse.

Three times with sighs she gives her sorrow fire
Ere once she can discharge one word of woe;   1605
At length addressed to answer his desire,
She modestly prepares to let them know
Her honor is ta'en prisoner by the foe;
  While Collatine and his consorted lords
  With sad attention long to hear her words.   1610

And now this pale swan in her wat'ry nest
Begins the sad dirge of her certain ending.
"Few words," quoth she, "shall fit the trespass best,
Where no excuse can give the fault amending:
In me moe woes than words are now depending;   1615
  And my laments would be drawn out too long,
  To tell them all with one poor tired tongue.

"Then be this all the task it hath to say:
Dear husband, in the interest of thy bed
A stranger came, and on that pillow lay   1620
Where thou wast wont to rest thy weary head;
And what wrong else may be imagined
  By foul enforcement might be done to me,
  From that, alas, thy Lucrece is not free.

"For in the dreadful dead of dark midnight,   1625
With shining falchion in my chamber came
A creeping creature with a flaming light,
And softly cried 'Awake, thou Roman dame,
And entertain my love; else lasting shame
  On thee and thine this night I will inflict,   1630
  If thou my love's desire do contradict.

1633. **yoke . . . will:** willingly submit to my desires.

1639. **start:** tremble.

1645. **adulterate:** adulterous.

1651. **purloined his eyes:** taken his eyes; i.e., completely absorbed his interest.

1659. **poisoned closet:** polluted body; **endure:** exist.

"'For some hard-favored groom of thine,' quoth he,
'Unless thou yoke thy liking to my will,
I'll murder straight, and then I'll slaughter thee,
And swear I found you where you did fulfill   1635
The loathsome act of lust, and so did kill
    The lechers in their deed: this act will be
    My fame, and thy perpetual infamy.'

"With this, I did begin to start and cry,
And then against my heart he set his sword,   1640
Swearing, unless I took all patiently,
I should not live to speak another word;
So should my shame still rest upon record,
    And never be forgot in mighty Rome
    Th'adulterate death of Lucrece and her groom.   1645

"Mine enemy was strong, my poor self weak,
And far the weaker with so strong a fear.
My bloody judge forbade my tongue to speak;
No rightful plea might plead for justice there.
His scarlet lust came evidence to swear   1650
    That my poor beauty had purloined his eyes,
    And when the judge is robbed, the prisoner dies.

"O, teach me how to make mine own excuse!
Or, at the least, this refuge let me find:
Though my gross blood be stained with this abuse,   1655
Immaculate and spotless is my mind;
That was not forced; that never was inclined
    To accessory yieldings, but still pure
    Doth in her poisoned closet yet endure."

1660. **hopeless merchant:** a metaphor of a ship-wrecked merchant ship; i.e., there is no hope from this loss.

1667-71. **As through . . . past:** the description of Collatine's rushing sorrow is compared to the torrent pouring through passages between the piers of London Bridge.

1672. **make a saw:** push back and forth like a saw.

1674. **attendeth:** observes.

1675. **untimely frenzy:** unaccustomed agitation.

1678. **sensible:** sensitive.

1682. **attend me:** listen to me.

1683. **suddenly:** quickly.

Lo, here, the hopeless merchant of this loss,   1660
With head declined, and voice dammed up with woe,
With sad-set eyes and wreathed arms across,
From lips new waxen pale begins to blow
The grief away that stops his answer so;
     But, wretched as he is, he strives in vain;   1665
     What he breathes out his breath drinks up again.

As through an arch the violent roaring tide
Outruns the eye that doth behold his haste,
Yet in the eddy boundeth in his pride
Back to the strait that forced him on so fast,   1670
In rage sent out, recalled in rage, being past;
     Even so his sighs, his sorrows, make a saw,
     To push grief on and back the same grief draw.

Which speechless woe of his poor she attendeth
And his untimely frenzy thus awaketh: 1675
"Dear lord, thy sorrow to my sorrow lendeth
Another power; no flood by raining slaketh.
My woe too sensible thy passion maketh
     More feeling-painful. Let it then suffice
     To drown one woe, one pair of weeping eyes.   1680

"And for my sake, when I might charm thee so,
For she that was thy Lucrece, now attend me:
Be suddenly revenged on my foe,
Thine, mine, his own; suppose thou dost defend me
From what is past. The help that thou shalt lend me   1685
     Comes all too late, yet let the traitor die;
     For sparing justice feeds iniquity.

1690. **plight:** pledge.

1691. **venge:** avenge.

1697. **imposition:** duty laid upon them.

1698. **bewrayed:** identified.

1699. **said:** revealed.

1714-15. **No, no . . . giving:** no woman hereafter, using the excuse that her heart was not in it, can clear herself of guilt.

"But ere I name him, you fair lords," quoth she,
Speaking to those that came with Collatine,
"Shall plight your honorable faiths to me,　　　　　1690
With swift pursuit to venge this wrong of mine;
For 'tis a meritorious fair design
　　To chase injustice with revengeful arms:
　　Knights, by their oaths, should right poor ladies'
　　　harms."

At this request, with noble disposition　　　　　1695
Each present lord began to promise aid,
As bound in knighthood to her imposition,
Longing to hear the hateful foe bewrayed.
But she, that yet her sad task hath not said,
　　The protestation stops. "O, speak," quoth she,　　1700
　　"How may this forced stain be wiped from me?

"What is the quality of my offence,
Being constrained with dreadful circumstance?
May my pure mind with the foul act dispense,
My low-declined honor to advance?　　　　　1705
May any terms acquit me from this chance?
　　The poisoned fountain clears itself again;
　　And why not I from this compelled stain?"

With this, they all at once began to say,
Her body's stain her mind untainted clears;　　　1710
While with a joyless smile she turns away
The face, that map which deep impression bears
Of hard misfortune, carved in it with tears.
　　"No, no," quoth she, "no dame hereafter living
　　By my excuse shall claim excuse's giving."　　　1715

1719. **accents:** halting changes in her voice.

1720. **assays:** attempts.

1725. **bail:** release.

1728. **sprite:** spirit.

1728-29. **through . . . destiny:** by her death, Lucrece cancels the shame that would have been hers through the duration of her life.

1731. **crew:** companions.

1732. **Lucrece' father:** Lucretius.

1734. **Brutus:** a lord accompanying Collatine; not to be confused with the Brutus contemporary with Caesar.

1736. **held it in chase:** flowed after it.

1740. **late-sacked:** recently plundered; **vastly:** desolately.

The suicide of Lucrece. From Giovanni Boccaccio, *De mulieribus claris* (1506).

114

Here with a sigh, as if her heart would break,
She throws forth Tarquin's name: "He, he," she says,
But more than "he" her poor tongue could not speak;
Till after many accents and delays,
Untimely breathings, sick and short assays,   1720
    She utters this: "He, he, fair lords, 'tis he,
    That guides this hand to give this wound to me."

Even here she sheathed in her harmless breast
A harmful knife, that thence her soul unsheathed:
That blow did bail it from the deep unrest   1725
Of that polluted prison where it breathed.
Her contrite sighs unto the clouds bequeathed
    Her winged sprite and through her wounds doth fly
    Life's lasting date from canceled destiny.

Stone-still, astonished with this deadly deed,   1730
Stood Collatine and all his lordly crew;
Till Lucrece' father, that beholds her bleed,
Himself on her self-slaughtered body threw;
And from the purple fountain Brutus drew
    The murd'rous knife, and, as it left the place,   1735
    Her blood, in poor revenge, held it in chase;

And bubbling from her breast, it doth divide
In two slow rivers, that the crimson blood
Circles her body in on every side,
Who like a late-sacked island vastly stood   1740
Bare and unpeopled in this fearful flood.
    Some of her blood still pure and red remained,
    And some looked black, and that false Tarquin
        stained.

1745. **wat'ry rigol:** serum that separates from the red-blood clot.

1756. **progenitors:** forebears.

1761. **bare-boned death:** skeleton.

1766. **surcease:** cease.

About the mourning and congealed face
Of that black blood a wat'ry rigol goes,   1745
Which seems to weep upon the tainted place;
And ever since, as pitying Lucrece' woes,
Corrupted blood some watery token shows;
　　And blood untainted still doth red abide,
　　Blushing at that which is so putrified.   1750

"Daughter, dear daughter," old Lucretius cries,
"That life was mine which thou hast here deprived.
If in the child the father's image lies,
Where shall I live now Lucrece is unlived?
Thou wast not to this end from me derived.   1755
　　If children predecease progenitors,
　　We are their offspring, and they none of ours.

"Poor broken glass, I often did behold
In thy sweet semblance my old age new born;
But now that fair fresh mirror, dim and old,   1760
Shows me a bare-boned death by time outworn;
O, from thy cheeks my image thou hast torn,
　　And shivered all the beauty of my glass,
　　That I no more can see what once I was.

"O time, cease thou thy course and last no longer,   1765
If they surcease to be that should survive.
Shall rotten death make conquest of the stronger,
And leave the falt'ring feeble souls alive?
The old bees die, the young possess their hive.
　　Then live, sweet Lucrece, live again, and see   1770
　　Thy father die, and not thy father thee."

1773. **give . . . place:** let him now express his grief.

1774. **key-cold:** cold as the metal of a key; a proverbial expression.

1776. **counterfeits to die:** faints.

1780. **dumb arrest:** stoppage of his speech.

1781. **use control:** paralyze him.

1784. **so thick:** with such rapidity.

1791. **strife:** competition.

1797. **sorrow's interest:** right to mourn.

By this, starts Collatine as from a dream,
And bids Lucretius give his sorrow place;
And then in key-cold Lucrece' bleeding stream
He falls, and bathes the pale fear in his face,   1775
And counterfeits to die with her a space;
    Till manly shame bids him possess his breath,
    And live to be revenged on her death.

The deep vexation of his inward soul
Hath served a dumb arrest upon his tongue;   1780
Who, mad that sorrow should his use control
Or keep him from heart-easing words so long,
Begins to talk; but through his lips do throng
    Weak words, so thick come in his poor heart's aid
    That no man could distinguish what he said.   1785

Yet sometime "Tarquin" was pronounced plain,
But through his teeth, as if the name he tore.
This windy tempest, till it blow up rain,
Held back his sorrow's tide, to make it more;
At last it rains, and busy winds give o'er;   1790
    Then son and father weep with equal strife
    Who should weep most, for daughter or for wife.

The one doth call her his, the other his,
Yet neither may possess the claim they lay.
The father says "She's mine." "O, mine she is,"   1795
Replies her husband; "do not take away
My sorrow's interest; let no mourner say
    He weeps for her, for she was only mine,
    And only must be wailed by Collatine."

1801. **spilled:** destroyed.

1803. **owed:** possessed.

1808. **emulation:** competition.

1813. **sportive:** amusing.

1815. **deep policy:** calculated shrewdness.

1807-15. **Brutus . . . disguise:** according to Ovid and Livy, Brutus had long pretended to be a sort of buffoon, entertaining the king's sons; he now threw off that disguise and came forward to avenge Lucrece.

1816. **armed . . . advisedly:** prepared his mind, not previously used, judiciously.

1819. **unsounded:** untried.

1820. **set . . . school:** give you, though you are well-experienced, some advice.

A Renaissance version of the Capitol at Rome, showing the medieval influences that had accrued in architecture, as in the classical legends, by Shakespeare's time. From Giovanni B. Marliani, *Urbis Romae typographia* (1588).

"O," quoth Lucretius, "I did give that life   1800
Which she too early and too late hath spilled."
"Woe, woe," quoth Collatine, "she was my wife;
I owed her, and 'tis mine that she hath killed."
"My daughter" and "my wife" with clamors filled
   The dispersed air, who, holding Lucrece' life,   1805
   Answered their cries, "my daughter" and "my wife."

Brutus, who plucked the knife from Lucrece' side,
Seeing such emulation in their woe,
Began to clothe his wit in state and pride,
Burying in Lucrece' wound his folly's show.   1810
He with the Romans was esteemed so
   As silly jeering idiots are with kings,
   For sportive words and utt'ring foolish things.

But now he throws that shallow habit by
Wherein deep policy did him disguise,   1815
And armed his long-hid wits advisedly
To check the tears in Collatinus' eyes.
"Thou wronged lord of Rome," quoth he, "arise;
   Let my unsounded self, supposed a fool,
   Now set thy long-experienced wit to school.   1820

"Why, Collatine, is woe the cure for woe?
Do wounds help wounds, or grief help grievous
   deeds?
Is it revenge to give thyself a blow
For his foul act by whom thy fair wife bleeds?
Such childish humor from weak minds proceeds.   1825
   Thy wretched wife mistook the matter so
   To slay herself, that should have slain her foe.

1828. **steep:** saturate.

1829. **dew of lamentations:** tears.

1832. **suffer:** permit.

1837. **fat earth's store:** rich earth's abundance.

1838. **country rights:** legal rights.

1844. **protestation:** oath.

1845. **allow:** confirm.

1849. **advised doom:** considered sentence.

1851. **thorough:** throughout.

1854. **plausibly:** commendably.

The banishment of Tarquin. From Livy, *Titus Livius* . . . *historicus duobus libris auctus* (1520).

"Courageous Roman, do not steep thy heart
In such relenting dew of lamentations,
But kneel with me and help to bear thy part   1830
To rouse our Roman gods with invocations
That they will suffer these abominations,
  Since Rome herself in them doth stand disgraced,
  By our strong arms from forth her fair streets
    chased.

"Now by the Capitol that we adore,   1835
And by this chaste blood so unjustly stained,
By heaven's fair sun that breeds the fat earth's store,
By all our country rights in Rome maintained,
And by chaste Lucrece' soul that late complained
  Her wrongs to us, and by this bloody knife,   1840
  We will revenge the death of this true wife."

This said, he struck his hand upon his breast,
And kissed the fatal knife to end his vow,
And to his protestation urged the rest,
Who, wond'ring at him, did his words allow;   1845
Then jointly to the ground their knees they bow,
  And that deep vow which Brutus made before
  He doth again repeat, and that they swore.

When they had sworn to this advised doom,
They did conclude to bear dead Lucrece thence,   1850
To show her bleeding body thorough Rome,
And so to publish Tarquin's foul offence;
Which being done with speedy diligence,
  The Romans plausibly did give consent
  To Tarquin's everlasting banishment.   1855

"THE PHOENIX AND
THE TURTLE"

The verse form of "The Phoenix and the Turtle" is trochaic tetrameter.

||||||||||||||||||||||||||||||||||||||||

1-4. Let . . . obey: an unidentified bird (*of loudest lay*) will serve as the herald and trumpet to call the birds together.

2. sole Arabian tree: the one tree upon which the phoenix was accustomed to sit.

5. harbinger: screech owl.

6. precurrer of the fiend: precursor of the devil.

7. Augur: foreteller.

9. interdict: forbid.

10. fowl of tyrant wing: predatory bird.

12. Keep . . . strict: keep the funeral decorous.

14. That . . . can: that knows funeral music.

15. death-divining swan: the swan's song foretold its death.

16. requiem: here used as a musical service in honor of the dead; **lack his right:** perhaps meaning lest the requiem lack its proper dignity.

17. treble-dated crow: the crow was believed to be extremely long-lived, hence *treble-dated*.

18. sable gender: black progeny.

The Arabian bird, or legendary phoenix, was said to destroy itself by fire every five hundred years and rise again from its own ashes. From Arnold Freitag, *Mythologia ethica* (1579).

"THE PHOENIX AND THE TURTLE"

Let the bird of loudest lay,
On the sole Arabian tree,
Herald sad and trumpet be,
To whose sound chaste wings obey.

But thou shrieking harbinger,   5
Foul precurrer of the fiend,
Augur of the fever's end,
To this troop come thou not near!

From this session interdict
Every fowl of tyrant wing,   10
Save the eagle, feathered king:
Keep the obsequy so strict.

Let the priest in surplice white,
That defunctive music can,
Be the death-divining swan,   15
Lest the requiem lack his right.

And thou treble-dated crow,
That thy sable gender mak'st

18-19. That . . . tak'st: an allusion to a curious classical notion that the crow mated with its beak.

23-24. Phoenix . . . hence: refers to the mystical burning together of the phoenix and the turtle.

25. in twain: by two.

27. Two . . . none: though they were two individuals, yet they were fused as one by their love.

29. asunder: apart.

32. wonder: marvel.

34. right: love due to him.

36. mine: scholars dispute over the meaning of the word: one defines it as "a rich source of wealth"; another thinks it means "that each—in the other's eye—took the form or image of the other, each was the other's self."

37-38. Property . . . same: the peculiar qualities of each were dismayed to find that they had been merged in a single self and were no longer the same.

43-44. To . . . compounded: after being fused by their love, neither was the same as before, but they were *compounded* ("mingled") into a single essence.

Love and constancy: a pair of turtledoves. From George Vertue, *A Description of the Works of . . . Wenceslaus Hollar* (1759).

With the breath thou giv'st and tak'st,
'Mongst our mourners shalt thou go.   20

Here the anthem doth commence:
Love and constancy is dead;
Phoenix and the turtle fled
In a mutual flame from hence.

So they loved, as love in twain   25
Had the essence but in one;
Two distincts, division none:
Number there in love was slain.

Hearts remote, yet not asunder;
Distance, and no space was seen   30
'Twixt this turtle and his queen:
But in them it were a wonder.

So between them love did shine,
That the turtle saw his right
Flaming in the phoenix' sight;   35
Either was the other's mine.

Property was thus appalled,
That the self was not the same;
Single nature's double name
Neither two nor one was called.   40

Reason, in itself confounded,
Saw division grow together,
To themselves yet either neither,
Simple were so well compounded;

45-48. That . . . remain: reason cried "How true seems this harmonious (*concordant*) couple. Love is right, but reason appears wrong, if that which is divisible remains as one."

49. threne: dirge.

51. Co-supremes: equals in greatness.

52. chorus . . . scene: commentary on their dissolving in flame.

Threnos: same as *threne;* dirge, elegiac song.

59-61. Leaving . . . chastity: because their union was chaste, it was no imperfection in them that they had no young.

65. urn: funeral urn containing the ashes of the phoenix and the turtle.

Fortune filling one cup for two lovers, symbolizing an equal fate for both. From Octavio van Veen, *Amorum emblemata* (1608).

That it cried, "How true a twain   45
Seemeth this concordant one!
Love hath reason, reason none,
If what parts can so remain."

Whereupon it made this threne
To the phoenix and the dove,   50
Co-supremes and stars of love,
As chorus to their tragic scene.

THRENOS

Beauty, truth, and rarity,
Grace in all simplicity,
Here enclosed, in cinders lie.   55

Death is now the phoenix' nest;
And the turtle's loyal breast
To eternity doth rest.

Leaving no posterity,
'Twas not their infirmity,   60
It was married chastity.

Truth may seem, but cannot be;
Beauty brag, but 'tis not she;
Truth and beauty buried be.

To this urn let those repair   65
That are either true or fair;
For these dead birds sigh a prayer.

VERSES FROM

THE PASSIONATE PILGRIM

1. This sonnet is a version of Sonnet 138. See *Shake-speare's Sonnets,* edited by Louis B. Wright and Virginia LaMar (Washington Square Press), p. 138.

VERSES FROM

THE PASSIONATE PILGRIM

Of the twenty poems in *The Passionate Pilgrim,*
the five generally attributed to Shakespeare are
printed below with the numbers given them in the
original edition.

1

WHEN my love swears that she is made of truth,
I do believe her, though I know she lies,
That she might think me some untutored youth,
Unskillful in the world's false forgeries.
Thus vainly thinking that she thinks me young,   5
Although I know my years be past the best,
I smiling credit her false-speaking tongue,
Outfacing faults in love with love's ill rest.
But wherefore says my love that she is young?
And wherefore say not I that I am old?   10
O, love's best habit's in a soothing tongue,
And age in love loves not to have years told.
   Therefore I'll lie with love, and love with me,
   Since that our faults in love thus smothered be.

2. This sonnet is a version of Sonnet 144. See *Shake-speare's Sonnets*, Wright-LaMar edition, p. 144.

2

Two loves I have, of comfort and despair,
That like two spirits do suggest me still;
My better angel is a man right fair,
My worser spirit a woman colored ill.
To win me soon to hell, my female evil   5
Tempteth my better angel from my side,
And would corrupt my saint to be a devil,
Wooing his purity with her fair pride.
And whether that my angel be turned fiend,
Suspect I may, yet not directly tell;   10
For being both to me, both to each friend,
I guess one angel in another's hell.
    The truth I shall not know, but live in doubt,
    Till my bad angel fire my good one out.

3. This is a variant of a sonnet appearing in *Love's Labor's Lost* (IV, iii, 62-75). See *Love's Labor's Lost,* edited by Louis B. Wright and Virginia LaMar (Washington Square Press), pp. 53-54.

3

Did not the heavenly rhetoric of thine eye,
'Gainst whom the world could not hold argument,
Persuade my heart to this false perjury?
Vows for thee broke deserve not punishment.
A woman I forswore; but I will prove,   5
Thou being a goddess, I forswore not thee:
My vow was earthly, thou a heavenly love;
Thy grace being gained cures all disgrace in me.
My vow was breath, and breath a vapor is;
Then, thou fair sun, that on this earth doth shine,   10
Exhal'st this vapor-vow; in thee it is:
If broken, then it is no fault of mine.
   If by me broke, what fool is not so wise
   To break an oath, to win a paradise?

5. This is a variant of a sonnet in *Love's Labor's Lost* (IV, ii, 120-139). See Wright-LaMar edition, p. 49.

"Thine eye Jove's lightning seems, thy voice his dreadful thunder"
From Vincenzo Cartari, *Imagini de gli dei delli antichi* (1615).

5

If love make me forsworn, how shall I swear to love?
O never faith could hold, if not to beauty vowed:
Though to myself forsworn, to thee I'll constant prove;
Those thoughts, to me like oaks, to thee like osiers
    bowed.
Study his bias leaves, and makes his book thine eyes,   5
Where all those pleasures live that art can
    comprehend.
If knowledge be the mark, to know thee shall suffice;
Well learned is that tongue that well can thee
    commend:
All ignorant that soul that sees thee without wonder;
Which is to me some praise, that I thy parts admire.   10
Thine eye Jove's lightning seems, thy voice his
    dreadful thunder,
Which, not to anger bent, is music and sweet fire.
  Celestial as thou art, O do not love that wrong,
    To sing heaven's praise with such an earthly
    tongue.

16. This is a variant of a lyrical passage in *Love's Labor's Lost* (IV, iii, 108-127). See Wright-LaMar edition, pp. 55-56.

16

On a day, alack the day!
Love, whose month was ever May,
Spied a blossom passing fair,
Playing in the wanton air.
Through the velvet leaves the wind   5
All unseen 'gan passage find,
That the lover, sick to death,
Wished himself the heaven's breath,
"Air," quoth he, "thy cheeks may blow;
Air, would I might triumph so!   10
But, alas! my hand hath sworn
Ne'er to pluck thee from thy thorn;
Vow, alack! for youth unmeet,
Youth, so apt to pluck a sweet.
Thou for whom Jove would swear   15
Juno but an Ethiope were;
And deny himself for Jove,
Turning mortal for thy love."

"A LOVER'S COMPLAINT"

The verse form of "A Lover's Complaint" is rhyme royal.

||||||||||||||||||||||||||||||||||||||||||

1. **reworded:** re-echoed.

2. **sist'ring vale:** neighboring valley.

3. **spirits . . . accorded:** his spirit was willing to listen to this voice and its echo.

5. **fickle:** unstable.

6. **atwain:** apart.

7. **wind and rain:** sighs and tears.

10. **thought:** thinker.

11. **carcass . . . done:** the mere shell of a beauty, now worn and spent.

12-13. **Time . . . quit:** time had not completely cut away all of youth, nor was youth all finished.

13. **fell:** cruel.

14. **seared:** withered.

15. **napkin:** handkerchief; **eyne:** eyes.

16. **conceited:** curiously wrought.

19. **And . . . bears:** her woe can be read in her tear-soaked handkerchief.

20. **undistinguished woe:** inarticulate grief.

"A LOVER'S COMPLAINT"

From off a hill whose concave womb reworded
A plaintful story from a sist'ring vale,
My spirits t'attend this double voice accorded,
And down I laid to list the sad-tuned tale,
Ere long espied a fickle maid full pale,   5
Tearing of papers, breaking rings atwain,
Storming her world with sorrow's wind and rain.

Upon her head a platted hive of straw,
Which fortified her visage from the sun,
Whereon the thought might think sometime it saw   10
The carcass of a beauty spent and done.
Time had not scythed all that youth begun,
Nor youth all quit, but spite of heaven's fell rage
Some beauty peeped through lattice of seared age.

Oft did she heave her napkin to her eyne,   15
Which on it had conceited characters,
Laund'ring the silken figures in the brine
That seasoned woe had pelleted in tears,
And often reading what contents it bears;
As often shrieking undistinguished woe,   20
In clamors of all size, both high and low.

22-23. Sometimes . . . intend: she raised her leveled eyes as a cannoneer would raise his gun, aiming as if to fire at the stars.

24-28. Sometime . . . commixed: the poet here describes her wandering eyes and distracted look; **commixed:** blended.

29-35. Her hair . . . negligence: her hair, only partially tied up, strings down in a disheveled manner.

31. sheaved: straw.

32. pined: anguished.

33. threaden fillet: ribbon for her hair.

36. maund: hand basket.

39. weeping margent: watery shore.

40. Like . . . wet: her tears add moisture to a place already too wet.

42. Where . . . all: where need petitions for some, but where abundance begs for everything.

43. schedules: papers containing writing.

45. posied: covered with mottoes.

47. moe: more.

48. sleided silk: silk in threads; **feat and affectedly:** delicately and with tender care.

Sometimes her leveled eyes their carriage ride,
As they did batt'ry to the spheres intend;
Sometime diverted their poor balls are tied
To th'orbed earth; sometimes they do extend   25
Their view right on; anon their gazes lend
To every place at once, and nowhere fixed,
The mind and sight distractedly commixed.

Her hair, nor loose nor tied in formal plat,
Proclaimed in her a careless hand of pride;   30
For some, untucked, descended her sheaved hat,
Hanging her pale and pined cheek beside;
Some in her threaden fillet still did bide,
And, true to bondage, would not break from thence,
Though slackly braided in loose negligence.   35

A thousand favors from a maund she drew
Of amber, crystal, and of beaded jet,
Which one by one she in a river threw,
Upon whose weeping margent she was set;
Like usury applying wet to wet,   40
Or monarchs' hands that lets not bounty fall
Where want cries some, but where excess begs all.

Of folded schedules had she many a one,
Which she perused, sighed, tore, and gave the flood;
Cracked many a ring of posied gold and bone,   45
Bidding them find their sepulchers in mud;
Found yet moe letters sadly penned in blood,
With sleided silk feat and affectedly
Enswathed and sealed to curious secrecy.

50. **fluxive:** flowing (with tears).

53. **unapproved:** unconfirmed by proof.

55. **rents:** rends; tears.

57. **reverend:** respected because of his age.

58. **ruffle:** hurlyburly; commotion.

59-60. **had . . . hours:** was past his prime.

61. **Towards . . . drew:** he quickly approached this sorrowing mind.

64. **grained bat:** staff which shows the grain of the wood; the meaning seems to be that, grasping his staff, he slid to the ground.

65. **comely:** decorous; decent.

67. **divide:** share.

68. **aught:** anything.

69. **suffering . . . assuage:** ease the madness of her sorrow.

72. **blasting:** blighting.

These often bathed she in her fluxive eyes, 50
And often kissed, and often 'gan to tear;
Cried, "O false blood, thou register of lies,
What unapproved witness dost thou bear!
Ink would have seemed more black and damned
    here!"
This said, in top of rage the lines she rents, 55
Big discontent so breaking their contents.

A reverend man that grazed his cattle nigh,
Sometime a blusterer that the ruffle knew
Of court, of city, and had let go by
The swiftest hours observed as they flew, 60
Towards this afflicted fancy fastly drew;
And, privileged by age, desires to know
In brief the grounds and motives of her woe.

So slides he down upon his grained bat,
And comely distant sits he by her side; 65
When he again desires her, being sat,
Her grievance with his hearing to divide.
If that from him there may be aught applied
Which may her suffering ecstasy assuage,
'Tis promised in the charity of age. 70

"Father," she says, "though in me you behold
The injury of many a blasting hour,
Let it not tell your judgment I am old:
Not age, but sorrow, over me hath power.
I might as yet have been a spreading flower, 75
Fresh to myself, if I had self-applied
Love to myself, and to no love beside.

80. **nature's outwards:** outward appearance.

81. **maidens' . . . face:** the girls could not keep their eyes off his face.

84. **deified:** glorified.

87. **parcels:** strands of hair.

88. **What's . . . find:** what's pleasant to do will find doers; taken with the following lines, it may mean that the many maidens who saw him found pleasure in the sight.

91. **largeness:** the largest imagination; **sawn:** seen.

93. **phoenix:** rare; scarce.

94. **termless:** youthful.

95. **Whose . . . wear:** whose naked smoothness claimed to be prettier than his newly-grown, downy whiskers.

96. **Yet . . . dear:** yet his face appeared more dear because of its ornament.

100. **maiden-tongued:** soft-spoken; **thereof free:** free of tongue; talkative.

104. **authorized youth:** sanction of youth.

105. **Did . . . truth:** dressed his falseness in the garb of truth.

"But woe is me! Too early I attended
A youthful suit—it was to gain my grace—
O, one by nature's outwards so commended   80
That maidens' eyes stuck over all his face.
Love lacked a dwelling and made him her place;
And when in his fair parts she did abide,
She was new lodged and newly deified.

"His browny locks did hang in crooked curls;   85
And every light occasion of the wind
Upon his lips their silken parcels hurls.
What's sweet to do, to do will aptly find:
Each eye that saw him did enchant the mind;
For on his visage was in little drawn   90
What largeness thinks in Paradise was sawn.

"Small show of man was yet upon his chin;
His phoenix down began but to appear,
Like unshorn velvet, on that termless skin,
Whose bare out-bragged the web it seemed to wear;   95
Yet showed his visage by that cost more dear;
And nice affections wavering stood in doubt
If best were as it was, or best without.

"His qualities were beauteous as his form,
For maiden-tongued he was, and thereof free;   100
Yet if men moved him, was he such a storm
As oft 'twixt May and April is to see,
When winds breathe sweet, unruly though they be.
His rudeness so with his authorized youth
Did livery falseness in a pride of truth.   105

107. **mettle:** spirit.

108. **sway:** dominance.

111-12. **Whether . . . steed:** whether the horse performed well thanks to his rider's skill or whether the rider handled the horse successfully because of the horse's training.

114. **habitude:** personality.

115. **appertainings:** belongings.

116. **not in his case:** not by appearance alone.

118. **for:** as.

119. **Pieced:** filled out.

122. **replication:** reply.

126. **craft of will:** capacity for influencing others.

130. **haunted:** frequented.

"Well could he ride, and often men would say,
'That horse his mettle from his rider takes:
Proud of subjection, noble by the sway,
What rounds, what bounds, what course, what stop
    he makes!'
And controversy hence a question takes,   110
Whether the horse by him became his deed,
Or he his manage by th'well-doing steed.

"But quickly on this side the verdict went:
His real habitude gave life and grace
To appertainings and to ornament,   115
Accomplished in himself, not in his case.
All aids, themselves made fairer by their place,
Came for additions; yet their purposed trim
Pieced not his grace, but were all graced by him.

"So on the tip of his subduing tongue   120
All kind of arguments and question deep,
All replication prompt, and reason strong,
For his advantage still did wake and sleep.
To make the weeper laugh, the laugher weep,
He had the dialect and different skill,   125
Catching all passions in his craft of will,

"That he did in the general bosom reign
Of young, of old, and sexes both enchanted,
To dwell with him in thoughts, or to remain
In personal duty, following where he haunted.   130
Consents bewitched, ere he desire, have granted,
And dialogued for him what he would say,
Asked their own wills, and made their wills obey.

140. **owe:** own.

144. **was . . . fee-simple:** had complete power to do as I wished.

148. **equals:** contemporaries.

156. **assay:** try.

157. **forced:** earnestly considered; **content:** desires.

"Many there were that did his picture get,
To serve their eyes, and in it put their mind;   135
Like fools that in th'imagination set
The goodly objects which abroad they find
Of lands and mansions, theirs in thought assigned;
And laboring in moe pleasures to bestow them
Than the true gouty landlord which doth owe them.   140

"So many have, that never touched his hand,
Sweetly supposed them mistress of his heart.
My woeful self, that did in freedom stand,
And was my own fee-simple, not in part,
What with his art in youth, and youth in art,   145
Threw my affections in his charmed power
Reserved the stalk and gave him all my flower.

"Yet did I not, as some my equals did,
Demand of him, nor being desired yielded;
Finding myself in honor so forbid,   150
With safest distance I mine honor shielded.
Experience for me many bulwarks builded
Of proofs new-bleeding, which remained the foil
Of this false jewel, and his amorous spoil.

"But ah, who ever shunned by precedent   155
The destined ill she must herself assay?
Or forced examples, 'gainst her own content,
To put the by-past perils in her way?
Counsel may stop awhile what will not stay;
For when we rage, advice is often seen   160
By blunting us to make our wills more keen.

162. **blood:** passion.
164. **forbod:** forbidden.
165. **in our behoof:** for our benefit.
167. **The one:** i.e., appetite.
173. **brokers:** agents.
185. **acture:** action.

"Nor gives it satisfaction to our blood
That we must curb it upon others' proof,
To be forbod the sweets that seems so good
For fear of harms that preach in our behoof.   165
O appetite, from judgment stand aloof!
The one a palate hath that needs will taste,
Though Reason weep, and cry it is thy last.

"For further I could say this man's untrue,
And knew the patterns of his foul beguiling;   170
Heard where his plants in others' orchards grew;
Saw how deceits were gilded in his smiling;
Knew vows were ever brokers to defiling;
Thought characters and words merely but art,
And bastards of his foul adulterate heart.   175

"And long upon these terms I held my city,
Till thus he 'gan besiege me: 'Gentle maid,
Have of my suffering youth some feeling pity,
And be not of my holy vows afraid.
That's to ye sworn to none was ever said;   180
For feasts of love I have been called unto,
Till now did ne'er invite nor never woo.

"'All my offences that abroad you see
Are errors of the blood, none of the mind;
Love made them not; with acture they may be,   185
Where neither party is nor true nor kind.
They sought their shame that so their shame did find;
And so much less of shame in me remains
By how much of me their reproach contains.

192. **teen:** pain.

193. **leisures:** leisure hours.

195. **in liveries:** in servitude.

204. **talents . . . hair:** locks of their hair.

205. **With . . . empleached:** with twisted gold lovingly interwoven.

206. **many . . . fair:** many individual fair ones.

208. **annexions:** things annexed.

209. **amplify:** explain in detail.

212. **invised:** a coined word, perhaps invisible.

214. **amend:** improve; gazing on an emerald was believed good for the eyesight.

217. **blazoned:** adorned.

"'Among the many that mine eyes have seen,   190
Not one whose flame my heart so much as warmed,
Or my affection put to the smallest teen,
Or any of my leisures ever charmed.
Harm have I done to them, but ne'er was harmed;
Kept hearts in liveries, but mine own was free,   195
And reigned commanding in his monarchy.

"'Look here what tributes wounded fancies sent me,
Of paled pearls and rubies red as blood;
Figuring that they their passions likewise lent me
Of grief and blushes, aptly understood   200
In bloodless white and the encrimsoned mood;
Effects of terror and dear modesty,
Encamped in hearts, but fighting outwardly.

"'And, lo, behold these talents of their hair,
With twisted metal amorously empleached,   205
I have received from many a several fair,
Their kind acceptance weepingly beseeched,
With the annexions of fair gems enriched,
And deep-brained sonnets that did amplify
Each stone's dear nature, worth, and quality.   210

"'The diamond, why, 'twas beautiful and hard,
Whereto his invised properties did tend;
The deep-green em'rald, in whose fresh regard
Weak sights their sickly radiance do amend;
The heaven-hued sapphire and the opal blend   215
With objects manifold; each several stone,
With wit well blazoned, smiled, or made some moan.

223. **must . . . be:** must be a sacrifice to you.

224. **you enpatron me:** you are the patron to whom the altar was erected.

225. **phraseless:** indescribable.

231. **distract:** separate.

235. **havings:** endowments.

236. **spirits of richest coat:** nobles with excellent coats-of-arms.

241. **Paling:** fencing off.

242. **gyves:** shackles.

"'Lo, all these trophies of affections hot,
Of pensived and subdued desires the tender,
Nature hath charged me that I hoard them not,   220
But yield them up where I myself must render,
That is, to you, my origin and ender;
For these, of force, must your oblations be,
Since I their altar, you enpatron me.

"'O then advance of yours that phraseless hand   225
Whose white weighs down the airy scale of praise;
Take all these similes to your own command,
Hallowed with sighs that burning lungs did raise;
What me your minister for you obeys
Works under you; and to your audit comes   230
Their distract parcels in combined sums.

"'Lo, this device was sent me from a nun,
Or sister sanctified, of holiest note,
Which late her noble suit in court did shun,
Whose rarest havings made the blossoms dote;   235
For she was sought by spirits of richest coat,
But kept cold distance, and did thence remove
To spend her living in eternal love.

"'But, O my sweet, what labor is't to leave
The thing we have not, mast'ring what not strives,   240
Paling the place which did no form receive,
Playing patient sports in unconstrained gyves!
She that her fame so to herself contrives,
The scars of battle scapeth by the flight,
And makes her absence valiant, not her might.   245

251. **immured:** put behind walls; cloistered.
258. **congest:** heap up.
259. **physic:** move.
273. **aloes:** bitterness.

"'O pardon me in that my boast is true!
The accident which brought me to her eye
Upon the moment did her force subdue,
And now she would the caged cloister fly.
Religious love put out religion's eye.   250
Not to be tempted, would she be immured,
And now to tempt all liberty procured.

"'How mighty then you are, O hear me tell!
The broken bosoms that to me belong
Have emptied all their fountains in my well,   255
And mine I pour your ocean all among.
I strong o'er them, and you o'er me being strong,
Must for your victory us all congest,
As compound love to physic your cold breast.

"'My parts had pow'r to charm a sacred nun,   260
Who, disciplined, ay, dieted in grace,
Believed her eyes when they t'assail begun,
All vows and consecrations giving place,
O most potential love, vow, bond, nor space,
In thee hath neither sting, knot, nor confine,   265
For thou art all, and all things else are thine.

"'When thou impressest, what are precepts worth
Of stale example? When thou wilt inflame,
How coldly those impediments stand forth,
Of wealth, of filial fear, law, kindred, fame!   270
Love's arms are peace, 'gainst rule, 'gainst sense,
        'gainst shame.
And sweetens, in the suff'ring pangs it bears,
The aloes of all forces, shocks and fears.

279. **credent:** trusting.
281. **dismount:** let go (in weeping).
286. **Who:** i.e., the stream of tears.
293. **cleft:** divided.
294. **extincture:** end.
297. **daffed:** put off.
298. **civil:** decorous.

" 'Now all these hearts that do on mine depend,
Feeling it break, with bleeding groans they pine,   275
And supplicant their sighs to you extend,
To leave the batt'ry that you make 'gainst mine,
Lending soft audience to my sweet design,
And credent soul to that strong-bonded oath,
That shall prefer and undertake my troth.'   280

"This said, his wat'ry eyes he did dismount,
Whose sights till then were leveled on my face;
Each cheek a river running from a fount
With brinish current downward flowed apace.
O, how the channel to the stream gave grace!   285
Who glazed with crystal gate the glowing roses
That flame through water which their hue encloses.

"O father, what a hell of witchcraft lies
In the small orb of one particular tear!
But with the inundation of the eyes   290
What rocky heart to water will not wear?
What breast so cold that is not warmed here?
O cleft effect! cold modesty, hot wrath,
Both fire from hence and chill extincture hath.

"For lo, his passion, but an art of craft,   295
Even there resolved my reason into tears;
There my white stole of chastity I daffed,
Shook off my sober guards and civil fears;
Appear to him as he to me appears,
All melting; though our drops this diff'rence bore: 300
His poisoned me, and mine did him restore.

303. **cautels:** crafty devices.
307. **rank:** coarse.
309. **in his level:** within his range.
312. **veiled in them:** hidden in his subtle devices.
314. **luxury:** lust.
318. **unexperient:** inexperienced.
329. **pervert:** ruin; **reconciled:** purified.

"In him a plenitude of subtle matter,
Applied to cautels, all strange forms receives,
Of burning blushes or of weeping water,
Or swooning paleness; and he takes and leaves,   305
In either's aptness, as it best deceives,
To blush at speeches rank, to weep at woes,
Or to turn white and swoon at tragic shows;

"That not a heart which in his level came
Could scape the hail of his all-hurting aim,   310
Showing fair nature is both kind and tame;
And, veiled in them, did win whom he would maim.
Against the thing he sought he would exclaim;
When he most burned in heart-wished luxury,
He preached pure maid and praised cold chastity.   315

"Thus merely with the garment of a Grace
The naked and concealed fiend he covered,
That th'unexperient gave the tempter place,
Which, like a cherubin, above them hovered.
Who, young and simple, would not be so lovered?   320
Ay me, I fell, and yet do question make
What I should do again for such a sake.

"O, that infected moisture of his eye,
O, that false fire which in his cheek so glowed,
O, that forced thunder from his heart did fly,   325
O, that sad breath his spongy lungs bestowed,
O, all that borrowed motion, seeming owed,
Would yet again betray the fore-betrayed,
And new pervert a reconciled maid."

CRITICAL COMMENTARY ON THE POEMS

CRITICAL COMMENTARY ON
THE POEMS

A brief selection of a few outstanding critical comments on *The Poems* is given below. A more complete selection will be found in *A New Variorum Edition of Shakespeare: The Poems*, edited by Hyder E. Rollins (Philadelphia and London, 1938), pp. 476 ff.

SAMUEL T. COLERIDGE
From *Biographia Literaria* (1817)

In this investigation I could not ... do better, than keep before me the earliest work of the greatest genius, that perhaps human nature has yet produced, our *myriad-minded* Shakspeare. I mean the *Venus and Adonis*, and the *Lucrece;* works which give at once strong promises of the strength, and yet obvious proofs of the immaturity, of his genius. From these I abstracted the following marks, as characteristics of original poetic genius in general.

1. In the *Venus and Adonis,* the first and most obvious excellence is the perfect sweetness of the versification; its adaptation to the subject; and the power

displayed in varying the march of the words without passing into a loftier and more majestic rhythm, than was demanded by the thoughts, or permitted by the propriety of preserving a sense of melody predominant. The delight in richness and sweetness of sound, even to a faulty excess, if it be evidently original, and not the result of an easily imitable mechanism, I regard as a highly favorable promise in the compositions of a young man. "The man that hath not music in his soul" can indeed never be a genuine poet. Imagery (even taken from nature, much more when transplanted from books, as travels, voyages, and works of natural history); affecting incidents; just thoughts; interesting personal or domestic feelings; and with these the art of their combination or intertexture in the form of a poem; may all by incessant effort be acquired as a trade, by a man of talents and much reading, who, as I once before observed, has mistaken an intense desire of poetic reputation for a natural poetic genius; the love of the arbitrary end for a possession of the peculiar means. But the sense of musical delight, with the power of producing it, is a gift of imagination; and this together with the power of reducing multitude into unity of effect, and modifying a series of thoughts by some one predominant thought or feeling, may be cultivated and improved, but can never be learnt. It is in these that "Poeta nascitur non fit."

2. A second promise of genius is the choice of subjects very remote from the private interests and circumstances of the writer himself. At least I have

found, that where the subject is taken immediately
from the author's personal sensations and experiences,
the excellence of a particular poem is but an equivo-
cal mark, and often a fallacious pledge, of genuine
poetic power. We may perhaps remember the tale
of the statuary, who had acquired considerable reputation for the legs of his goddesses, though the rest
of the statue accorded but indifferently with ideal
beauty; till his wife elated by her husband's praises,
modestly acknowledged, that she herself had been his
constant model. In the *Venus and Adonis,* this proof
of poetic power exists even to excess. It is throughout
as if a superior spirit more intuitive, more intimately
conscious, even than the characters themselves, not
only of every outward look and act, but of the flux
and reflux of the mind in all its subtlest thoughts and
feelings, were placing the whole before our view;
himself meanwhile unparticipating in the passions,
and actuated only by that pleasurable excitement,
which had resulted from the energetic fervor of his
own spirit in so vividly exhibiting, what it had so
accurately and profoundly contemplated. I think, I
should have conjectured from these poems, that even
then the great instinct, which impelled the poet to
the drama, was secretly working in him, prompting
him by a series and never broken chain of imagery,
always vivid and because unbroken, often minute; by
the highest effort of the picturesque in words, of
which words are capable, higher perhaps than was
ever realized by any other poet, even Dante not ex-
cepted; to provide a substitute for that visual lan-

guage, that constant intervention and running comment by tone, look and gesture, which in his dramatic works he was entitled to expect from the players. His *Venus and Adonis* seem at once the characters themselves, and the whole representation of those characters by the most consummate actors. You seem to be *told* nothing, but to see and hear every thing. Hence it is, that from the perpetual activity of attention required on the part of the reader; from the rapid flow, the quick change, and the playful nature of the thoughts and images; and above all from the alienation, and, if I may hazard such an expression, the utter *aloofness* of the poet's own feelings, from those of which he is at once the painter and the analyst; that though the very subject cannot but detract from the pleasure of a delicate mind, yet never was poem less dangerous on a moral account. Instead of doing as Ariosto, and as, still more offensively, Wieland has done, instead of degrading and deforming passion into appetite, the trials of love into the struggles of concupiscence; Shakspeare has here represented the animal impulse itself, so as to preclude all sympathy with it, by dissipating the reader's notice among the thousand outward images, and now beautiful, now fanciful circumstances, which form its dresses and its scenery; or by diverting our attention from the main subject by those frequent witty or profound reflections, which the poet's ever active mind has deduced from, or connected with, the imagery and the incidents. The reader is forced into too much action to sympathize with the merely passive of our nature. As little can a mind thus roused and awakened be brooded on by mean and indistinct emotion, as the low, lazy mist can creep upon the surface of a lake, while a strong gale is driving it onward in waves and billows.

3. It has been before observed, that images however beautiful, though faithfully copied from nature, and as accurately represented in words, do not of themselves characterize the poet. They become proofs of original genius only as far as they are modified by a predominant passion; or by associated thoughts or images awakened by that passion; or when they have the effect of reducing multitude to unity, or succession to an instant; or lastly, when a human and intellectual life is transferred to them from the poet's own spirit. . . . It is by this, that [Shakespeare] . . . still gives a dignity and a passion to the objects which he presents. Unaided by any previous excitement, they burst upon us at once in life and in power. . . .

As of higher worth, so doubtless still more characteristic of poetic genius does the imagery become, when it moulds and colors itself to the circumstances, passion, or character, present and foremost in the mind. . . .

Scarcely less sure, or if a less valuable, not less indispensable mark . . . will the imagery supply, when, with more than the power of the painter, the poet gives us the liveliest image of succession with the feeling of simultaneousness!

With this he breaketh from the sweet embrace
Of those fair aims, that held him to her heart,
And homeward through the dark lawns runs apace:
Look how a bright star shooteth from the sky!
So glides he through the night from Venus' eye.

4. The last character I shall mention, which would prove indeed but little, except as taken conjointly with the former; yet without which the former could scarce exist in a high degree, and (even if this were possible) would give promises only of transitory flashes and a meteoric power; is DEPTH, and ENERGY of THOUGHT. No man was ever yet a great poet, without being at the same time a profound philosopher. For poetry is the blossom and the fragrancy of all human knowledge, human thoughts, human passions, emotions, language. In Shakspeare's *poems*, the creative power, and the intellectual energy wrestle as in a war embrace. Each in its excess of strength seems to threaten the extinction of the other. At length, in the DRAMA they were reconciled, and fought each with its shield before the breast of the other. Or like two rapid streams, that at their first meeting within narrow and rocky banks mutually strive to repel each other, and intermix reluctantly and in tumult; but soon finding a wider channel and more yielding shores blend, and dilate, and flow on in one current and with one voice. The *Venus and Adonis* did not perhaps allow the display of the deeper passions. But the story of Lucretia seems to favor, and even demand their intensest workings. And yet we find in *Shak-*

speare's management of the tale neither pathos, nor any other *dramatic* quality. There is the same minute and faithful imagery as in the former poem, in the same vivid colours, inspirited by the same impetuous vigour of thought, and diverging and contracting with the same activity of the assimilative and of the modifying faculties; and with a yet larger display, a yet wider range of knowledge and reflection; and lastly, with the same perfect dominion, often *domination*, over the whole world of language. What then shall we say? even this; that Shakspeare, no mere child of nature; no automaton of genius; no passive vehicle of inspiration possessed by the spirit, not possessing it; first studied patiently, meditated deeply, understood minutely, till knowledge become habitual and intuitive wedded itself to his habitual feelings, and at length gave birth to that stupendous power, by which he stands alone, with no equal or second in his own class; to that power, which seated him on one of the two glory-smitten summits of the poetic mountain, with Milton as his compeer not rival. While the former darts himself forth, and passes into all the forms of human character and passion, the one Proteus of the fire and the flood; the other attracts all forms and things to himself, into the unity of his own IDEAL. All things and modes of action shape themselves anew in the being of MILTON; while SHAKSPEARE becomes all things, yet for ever remaining himself.

F. P. G. GUIZOT
From *Shakespeare and His Times* (1852)

[*Venus and Adonis* needs] to be excused, it must be confessed, by the effervescence of a youth too much addicted to dreams of pleasure not to attempt to reproduce them in all their forms. In *Venus and Adonis*, the poet, absolutely carried away by the voluptuous power of his subject, seems entirely to have lost sight of its mythological wealth. Venus, stripped of the prestige of divinity, is nothing but a beautiful courtesan, endeavoring unsuccessfully, by all the prayers, tears, and artifices of love, to stimulate the languid desires of a cold and disdainful youth. Hence arises a monotony which is not redeemed by the simple gracefulness and poetic merit of many passages, and which is augmented by the division of the poem into stanzas of six lines, the last two of which almost invariably present a *jeu d'esprit*. But a metre singularly free from irregularities, a cadence full of harmony, and a versification which had never before been equaled in England, announced the "honey-tongued poet," and the poem of *Lucrece* appeared soon afterward to complete those epic productions which for some time sufficed to maintain his glory.

After having, in *Venus and Adonis*, employed the most lascivious colors to depict the pangs of unsatisfied desire, Shakspeare has described, in *The Rape of Lucrece*, with the chastest pen, and by way of reparation, as it were, the progress and triumph of

criminal lust. The refinement of the ideas, the affecta-
tion of the style, and the merits of the versification,
are the same in both works; the poetry in the second
is less brilliant, but more emphatic, and abounds
less in graceful images than in lofty thoughts; but we
can already discern indications of a profound acquaintance with the feelings of man, and great talent
in developing them in a dramatic form, by means of
the slightest circumstances of life. Thus Lucrece,
weighed down by a sense of her shame, after a night
of despair, summons a young slave at dawn of day,
to dispatch him to the camp with a letter to call her
husband home; the slave, being of a timid and simple
character, blushes on appearing in the presence of
his mistress; but Lucrece, filled with the consciousness
of her dishonor, imagines that he blushes at her
shame; and, under the influence of the idea that her
secret is discovered, she stands trembling and confused before her slave.

H. A. TAINE
From *History of English Literature,*
tr. by H. Van Laun (1871)

Outside the theatre he lived with fashionable young
nobles, Pembroke, Montgomery, Southampton, and
others, whose hot and licentious youth fed his imagination and senses by the example of Italian pleasures
and elegances. Add to this the rapture and transport

of poetical nature, and this afflux, this boiling over
of all the powers and desires which takes place in
brains of this kind, when the world for the first time
opens before them, and you will understand the
Venus and Adonis, "the first heir of his invention."
In fact, it is a first cry, a cry in which the whole man
is displayed. Never was seen a heart so quivering to
the touch of beauty, of beauty of every kind, so
ravished with the freshness and splendour of things,
so eager and so excited in adoration and enjoyment,
so violently and entirely carried to the very limit of
voluptuousness. His Venus is unique; no painting of
Titian's has a more brilliant and delicious colouring;
no strumpet-goddess of Tintoret or Giorgione is more
soft and beautiful. . . . All is taken by storm, the
senses first, the eyes dazzled by carnal beauty, but
the heart also from whence the poetry overflows;
the fulness of youth inundates even inanimate things;
the landscape looks charming amidst the rays of the
rising sun, the air, saturated with brightness, makes a
gala-day:

"Lo, here the gentle lark, weary of rest,
From his moist cabinet mounts up on high,
And wakes the morning, from whose silver breast
The sun ariseth in his majesty;
Who doth the world so gloriously behold
That cedar-tops and hills seem burnish'd gold."

An admirable debauch of imagination and rapture,
yet disquieting; for such a mood will carry one a long

way. No fair and frail dame in London was without *Adonis* on her table. Perhaps he perceived that he had transcended the bounds, for the tone of his next poem, the *Rape of Lucrece,* is quite different; but as he had already a spirit wide enough to embrace at the same time, as he did afterwards in his dramas, the two extremes of things, he continued none the less to follow his bent. The "sweet abandonment of love" was the great occupation of his life; he was tender-hearted, and he was a poet: nothing more is required to be smitten, deceived, to suffer, to traverse without pause the circle of illusions and pains, which whirls and whirls round, and never ends.

GEORG BRANDES
From *William Shakespeare,*
tr. by William Archer et al (1898)

In *Venus and Adonis* glows the whole fresh sensuousness of the Renaissance and of Shakespeare's youth. . . .

The conduct of the poem presents a series of opportunities and pretexts for voluptuous situations and descriptions. The ineffectual blandishments lavished by Venus on the chaste and frigid youth, who, in his sheer boyishness, is as irresponsive as a bashful woman—her kisses, caresses, and embraces, are depicted in detail. It is as though a Titian or Rubens had painted a model in a whole series of tender situations, now in one attitude, now in another. Then comes the suggestive scene in which Adonis's horse breaks away in order to meet the challenge of a mare which happens to wander by, together with the goddess's comments thereupon. Then new advances and solicitations, almost inadmissibly daring, according to the taste of our day.

An element of feeling is introduced in the portrayal of Venus's anguish when Adonis expresses his intention of hunting the boar. But it is to sheer description that the poet chiefly devotes himself—description of the charging boar, description of the fair young body bathed in blood, and so forth. There is a fire and rapture of colour in it all, as in a picture by some Italian master of a hundred years before.

Quite unmistakable is the insinuating, luscious, almost saccharine quality of the writing, which accounts for the fact that, when his immediate contemporaries speak of Shakespeare's diction, honey is the similitude that first suggests itself to them. . . .

There is, indeed, an extraordinary sweetness in these strophes. Tenderness, every here and there, finds really entrancing utterance. . . .

But the style also exhibits numberless instances of tasteless Italian artificiality. Breathing the "heavenly moisture" of Adonis's breath, she

"Wishes her cheeks were gardens full of flowers,
  So they were dew'd with such distilling showers."

Of Adonis's dimples it is said:—

"These lovely caves, these round enchanting pits,
  Open'd their mouths to swallow Venus' liking."

"My love to love," says Adonis, "is love but to disgrace
it." Venus enumerates the delights he would afford to
each of her senses separately, supposing her deprived
of all the rest, and concludes thus:—

" 'But, O, what banquet wert thou to the taste,
  Being nurse and feeder of the other four
  Would they not wish the feast might ever last,
  And bid Suspicion double-lock the door,
      Lest Jealousy, that sour unwelcome guest,
      Should, by his stealing in, disturb the feast?' "

Such lapses of taste are not infrequent in Shakespeare's early comedies as well. They answer, in their
way, to the riot of horrors in *Titus Andronicus*—
analogous mannerisms of an as yet undeveloped art.

At the same time, the puissant sensuousness of this
poem is as a prelude to the large utterance of passion
in *Romeo and Juliet*, and towards its close Shakespeare soars, so to speak, symbolically, from a de-
lineation of the mere fever of the senses to a forecast
of that love in which it is only one element, when he
makes Adonis say:—

" 'Love comforteth like sunshine after rain,
  But Lust's effect is tempest after sun;

Love's gentle spring doth always fresh remain,
Lust's winter comes ere summer half be done:
  Love surfeits not, Lust like a glutton dies;
  Love is all truth, Lust full of forged lies.' "

It would, of course, be absurd to lay too much stress
on these edifying antitheses in this unedifying poem.
It is more important to note that the descriptions of
animal life—for example, that of the hare's flight—
are unrivalled for truth and delicacy of observation,
and to mark how, even in his early work, Shakespeare's style now and then rises to positive
greatness. . . .

  [*Lucrece*] is designed as a counterpart to its prede-
cessor. The one treats of male, the other of female,
chastity. The one portrays ungovernable passion in a
woman; the other, criminal passion in a man. But in
Lucrece the theme is seriously and morally handled.
It is almost a didactic poem, dealing with the havoc
wrought by unbridled and brutish desire.

  It was not so popular in its own day as its prede-
cessor, and it does not afford the modern reader any
very lively satisfaction. It shows an advance in metri-
cal accomplishment. To the six-line stanza of *Venus
and Adonis* a seventh line is added, which heightens
its beauty and its dignity. The strength of *Lucrece*
lies in its graphic and gorgeous descriptions, and in
its sometimes microscopic psychological analysis. For
the rest, its pathos consists of elaborate and far-
fetched rhetoric.

  The lament of the heroine after the crime has been

committed is pure declamation, extremely eloquent no doubt, but copious and artificial as an oration of Cicero's, rich in apostrophes and antitheses. The sorrow of "Collatine and his consorted lords" is portrayed in laboured and quibbling speeches. Shakespeare's knowledge and mastery are most clearly seen in the reflections scattered through the narrative. . . .

A comparison between Ovid's style and that of Shakespeare certainly does not redound to the advantage of the modern poet. In opposition to this semi-barbarian, Ovid seems the embodiment of classic severity. Shakespeare's antithetical conceits and other lapses of taste are painfully obtrusive. Every here and there we come upon such stumbling-blocks as these:—

> "Some of her blood still pure and red remain'd,
> And some look'd black, and that false Tarquin
> stain'd;"

or,

> "If children pre-decease progenitors,
> We are their offspring, and they none of ours."

This lack of nature and of taste is not only characteristic of the age in general, but is bound up with the great excellences and rare capacities which Shakespeare was now developing with such amazing rapidity. His momentary leaning towards this style was due, in part at least, to the influence of his fellow-

poets, his friends, his rivals in public favour—the influence, in short, of that artistic microcosm in whose
atmosphere his genius shot up to sudden maturity. . . .

Shakespeare could not but strive from the first to
outdo his fellows in strength and skill. At last he
comes to think, like Hamlet: however deep they
dig—

> "it shall go hard
> But I will delve one yard below their mines"

—one of the most characteristic utterances of Hamlet
and of Shakespeare.

This sense of rivalry contributed to the formation
of Shakespeare's early manner, both in his narrative
poems and in his plays. Hence arose that straining
after subtleties, that absorption in quibbles, that wan-
toning in wordplays, that bandying to and fro of
shuttlecocks of speech. Hence, too, that state of over-
heated passion and over-stimulated fancy, in which
image begets image with a headlong fecundity, like
that of the low organisms which pullulate by mere
scission.

WALTER A. RALEIGH
Professor of Poetry, Oxford
From *Shakespeare* (1907)

[*Venus* and *Lucrece*] are, first of all, works of art.
They are poetic exercises by one who has set himself

to prove his craftsmanship upon a given subject. If traces of the prentice hand are visible, it is not in any uncertainty of execution, nor in any failure to achieve an absolute beauty, but rather in the very ostentation of artistic skill. There is no remission, at any point, from the sense of conscious art. The poems are as delicate as carved ivory, and as bright as burnished silver. They deal with disappointment, crime, passion, and tragedy, yet are destitute of feeling for the human situation, and are, in effect, painless. This painlessness, which made Hazlitt compare them to a couple of ice-houses, is due not to insensibility in the poet, but to his preoccupation with his art. He handles life from a distance, at two removes, and all the emotions awakened by the poems are emotions felt in the presence of art, not those suggested by life. The arts of painting and rhetoric are called upon to lend poetry their subjects and their methods. . . . It would not be rash to say outright that both the poems were suggested by pictures, and must be read and appreciated in the light of that fact. But the truth for criticism remains the same if they took their sole origin from the series of pictures painted in words by the master-hand of Ovid. "So workmanly the blood and tears are drawn."

The rhetorical art of the poems is no less manifest. The tirades and laments of both poems, on Love and Lust, on Night, and Time, and Opportunity, are exquisitely modulated rhetorical diversions; they express rage, sorrow, melancholy, despair; and it is all equally soothing and pleasant, like listening to a dreamy sonata. Lucrece, at the tragic crisis of her history, decorates her speech with far-fetched illustrations and the arabesques of a pensive fancy. And as if her own disputation of her case were not enough, the poet pursues her with "sentences," conveying appropriate moral reflections. She is sadder than ever when she hears the birds sing; and he is ready with the poetical statutes that apply to her case:

> 'Tis double death to drown in ken of shore;
> He ten times pines that pines beholding food;
> To see the salve doth make the wound ache more;
> Great grief grieves most at that would do it good.

There is no morality in the general scheme of these poems; the morality is all inlaid, making of the poem a rich mosaic. The plays have to do with a world too real to be included in a simple moral scheme; the poems with a world too artificial to be brought into any vital relation with morality. The main motive prompting the poet is the love of beauty for beauty's sake, and of wit for the exercise of wit.

EMILE LEGOUIS

From *A History of English Literature,*
tr. by Helen D. Irvine (1927)

[*Venus and Adonis*] eliminates nearly all the mythology. A powerful instinct impels him towards reality. His goddess is a woman skilled at lovemaking and ravaged by passion, and in Adonis we already have the young sport-loving Englishman, annoyed and fretted by the pursuit of a beautiful amorous courtesan whose sensuality is unbounded and who retains no prestige of divinity.

These realistic passions are framed by equally realistic pictures and episodes. The arguments of Venus are supported by the appearance of "a breeding jennet" rushing out of a neighbouring copse and at once joined by Adonis's steed, who breaks his rein in order to go to her. The horse is painted with dry precision, as by an expert. Further, the goddess vividly describes boar-hunting and hare-hunting to the youth, the one an over-dangerous sport whence she would dissuade him, the other a safe amusement which she recommends. These two specialised pictures are plainly drawn at first-hand and from observation, and the most touching lines of the poem tell of the agony of the "timorous flying hare."

It is, however, impossible not to recognise that the dominant note is struck by the voluptuous painting of the goddess's lascivious gestures and the complacent retailing of her glowing words. Thus regarded, the poem is, from the merely artistic point of view, a complete success. Shakespeare gives evidence in its stanzas of astonishing linguistic wealth and skill. He too is over-prone to conceits, but on the whole the critic has only to admire his masterliness.

Because he writes in stanzas, not, like Marlowe, in rhyming couplets, his poem has less the turn of a narrative than *Hero and Leander*. It is pre-eminently

a series of pictures. If the licentiousness of the two
poems is about equal, that of Shakespeare has the
advantage of dealing with a mythological legend and
staging a heroine neither of which could be much
profaned. On the other hand, his eroticism is more
elaborate and has less dash and spontaneity than
that of his rival.

It seems to have been for an artistic purpose that
Shakespeare in the following year chose the rape of
Lucretia as the subject of a poem which forms at
once a pendant and a contrast to the preceding one.
Having painted the attempt of an amorous woman
to seduce a youth, he proceeded to represent the
rape of a chaste wife by a wretched debauchee.

The later work shows increased power and breadth,
but the old defects in strengthened form. The speeches
are longer than ever and less appropriate—Lucrece's
supplications to Tarquin before his crime, the endless plaints which intervene between the assault and
the suicide of the outraged wife. The minute descriptions, with their prettiness and conceits, are especially
irritating, veiling and enervating, as they do, the
tragedy of the theme. In the portrait of Lucrece,
asleep upon her bed as Tarquin draws her curtains,
poetry and bad taste are inextricably mingled.

From end to end of the poem the reader is exas-
perated by the poet's very talent, his fancy and eloquence, and is brought to regret both Ovid's quieter
picture and Chaucer's artless rendering thereof. He
tells himself that the limits of the sonnet and restric-
tions of the theatre had the happy effect of setting

bounds to the poet's exuberance. An aspect of Shakespeare is revealed which could not appear so clearly in his other works, but it is on the whole the less pure side of his genius, both morally and poetically.

KEY TO FAMOUS LINES

KEY TO FAMOUS LINES

Venus and Adonis

Hunting he loved, but love he laughed to scorn.　　4

Ten kisses short as one, one long as twenty.　　22

Leading him prisoner in a red-rose chain.　　110

Were I hard-favored, foul, or wrinkled-old,　　133
Ill-nurtured, crooked, churlish, harsh in voice,
O'erworn, despised, rheumatic and cold,
Thick-sighted, barren, lean, and lacking juice,
　　Then mightst thou pause, for then I were not for thee;
　　But having no defects, why dost abhor me?

Love is a spirit all compact of fire,　　149
Not gross to sink, but light, and will aspire.

O, what a war of looks was then between them,　　355
Her eyes petitioners to his eyes suing!

The sea hath bounds, but deep desire hath none.　　389

A thousand kisses buys my heart from me;　　517
And pay them at thy leisure, one by one.

Foul words and frowns must not repel a lover;   573
What though the rose have prickles, yet 'tis plucked.
  Were beauty under twenty locks kept fast,
  Yet love breaks through, and picks them all at last.

This sour informer, this bate-breeding spy,   655
This canker that eats up Love's tender spring,
This carry-tale, dissentious Jealousy,
That sometime true news, sometime false doth bring.

Danger deviseth shifts; wit waits on fear.   690

The path is smooth that leadeth on to danger.   788

Call it not love, for Love to heaven is fled   793
Since sweating Lust on earth usurped his name.

Love comforteth like sunshine after rain,   799
But Lust's effect is tempest after sun;
Love's gentle spring doth always fresh remain,
Lust's winter comes ere summer half be done;
  Love surfeits not, Lust like a glutton dies;
  Love is all truth, Lust full of forged lies.

And, beauty dead, black chaos comes again.   1020

The grass stoops not, she treads on it so light.   1028

The Rape of Lucrece

Beauty itself doth of itself persuade   29
The eyes of men without an orator.

Who buys a minute's mirth to wail a week?   213
Or sells eternity to get a toy?

For princes are the glass, the school, the book,   615
Where subjects' eyes do learn, do read, do look.

Unruly blasts wait on the tender spring;   869
Unwholesome weeds take root with precious flowers:
The adder hisses where the sweet birds sing;
What virtue breeds iniquity devours.

The mightier man, the mightier is the thing   1004
That makes him honored or begets him hate;
For greatest scandal waits on greatest state.

True grief is fond and testy as a child.   1094

A woeful hostess brooks not merry guests.   1125

For men have marble, women waxen, minds.   1240

Though men can cover crimes with bold stern   1252
    looks,
Poor women's faces are their own faults' books.

It easeth some, though none it ever cured,   1581
To think their dolor others have endured.

For sparing justice feeds iniquity.   1687

Do wounds help wounds, or grief help grievous 1822
   deeds?